wondergirls

The Makeover

Jillian Brooks

SCHOLASTIC INC.
New York Toronto London Auckland Sydney
Mexico City New Delhi Hong Kong Buenos Aires

No part of this publication may be reproduced in whole or in part, or stored in a retrieval system or transmitted in any form by any means, electronic, mechanical, photocopying, recording, or otherwise, without written permission of the publisher. For information regarding permission, write to Scholastic Inc., Attention: Permissions Department, 557 Broadway, New York, NY 10012.

ISBN 0-439-35494-3

Copyright © 2003 17th Street Productions,
an Alloy, Inc. company
All rights reserved.
Published by Scholastic Inc.

 Produced by 17th Street Productions,
an Alloy, Inc. company
151 West 26th Street
New York, NY 10001

SCHOLASTIC and associated logos are trademarks and/or registered trademarks of Scholastic Inc.

12 11 10 9 8 7 6 5 4 3 2 1   3 4 5 6 7 8/0

Printed in the U.S.A.   40
First Scholastic printing, January 2003

chapter
ONE

Item on the front page of the Arts and Entertainment section of the Wonder Lake Daily Bee

**WONDER LAKE MIDDLE SCHOOL ORCHESTRA
BRINGS HOME THE SILVER**

The Wonder Lake Middle School Orchestra won second place overall in the semifinal regional orchestra competition last Sunday. They competed against fifteen other schools in the area and were bested only by three-time semifinal winner Collindale Middle School. Wonder Lake sixth grader Ryan Bradley won a first-place medal for best solo performance on the violin—

"Arielle, look out!"

Grabbing my lunch tray and heading into the cafeteria, I ducked as a rock-hard cafeteria roll whizzed by my head, missing me by inches. It sailed on to bonk Danny Parker, one of the goofier guys in our grade, on the head.

"I'll get you, Ryan!" he called in my direction. "You're asking for it now!"

I turned behind me, in the direction he'd been

1

calling, and came face-to-face with Ryan Bradley, class clown and all-around goofball. On rare occasions—*really* rare—Ryan can be funny, but mostly I find him kind of immature and silly.

"Sorry about that, Arielle," he apologized with a little crooked grin. "I wasn't aiming for you, I swear."

I sighed and straightened the juice box on my lunch tray. "All right, Ryan. But food fights are *so* fifth grade."

Ryan chuckled and headed for the end of the lunch line. "I'll remember that," he promised.

"Hey, Ryan," some kid called behind me, "did you just snag my roll?"

As Ryan walked away, I looked around the lunchroom, trying to get my bearings. My friends and I always sit at this one table by the window, and I looked over to see whether they were there yet.

"Arielle, over here!"

I smiled. There was my friend Felicia, sitting at the table and calling over to me. My other friends, Amanda Kepner and Traci McClintic, were sitting with her.

"Hi, guys!" I said happily as Amanda and Felicia scooted over to give me room on the bench. The four of us—me, Felicia, Amanda, and Traci—are best friends. We're in sixth grade at Wonder Lake Middle School, and we do just about everything together. This is the first year at middle school for all of us, but Amanda and I have known each other since we were little. We met Traci and Felicia at the beginning of the year, and the four of us just clicked. We get along great—most of the time.

"It's so good to have everybody back together again," I said, digging into my lunch: spaghetti and meatballs. Not my idea of fine cuisine, but I'd forgotten to pack my lunch that day.

"I know," Traci agreed. "I'm so glad to be home."

Felicia and Traci had been in Chicago for the last four days at this regional orchestra competition, where the Wonder Lake Middle School Orchestra had won second place. I was really proud of them.

"Me too," Felicia said. "Chicago was so cool, but I would rather have lunch with my best friends any day of the week."

"Aw, shucks, Feleesh," Amanda said, and we all laughed.

I was really glad that Felicia was back. We're all best friends, but I'm closer to Felicia and Amanda than I am to Traci. I love her, too, but we're kind of different. In fact, when Traci first moved here from Charleston, we used to fight a lot.

"Traci and Felicia were telling me about going to the top of the Sears Tower," Amanda told me.

"Oh, that must have been amazing," I said. "Isn't it like the tallest building in the world?"

"Yeah, almost," Traci said. "It's the second tallest. It was amazing up there. It felt like you could see the whole world."

"And it was so windy, for a second I felt like I could get blown right off the top," Felicia added.

"That sounds really cool," I said.

"So tell us how Healing Paws went," Traci said.

"Oh yeah, my dad said it was the best yet," Felicia said.

Healing Paws is a program we started that brings animals to the children's ward of Wonder Lake Hospital. It really cheers up the kids. We bring puppies, kittens, gerbils, and other animals from Felicia's dad's animal shelter. We also volunteer at the shelter once a week.

"It was great. We're really getting the hang of it now—only one puppy escaped on the hospital floor. We had to chase it all around, but that was actually pretty fun for the kids because they thought it was so hilarious," I told them.

"Nurse Julia didn't think it was very funny, though," Amanda said with a laugh. "She was yelling at us to 'get control of that little creature' and screaming every time it came near her."

We all laughed. I could totally replay the scene in my mind—it had been a definite highlight. My friends are all *really* into animals. Animals are okay, I guess, but I don't get as excited about them. As cute as puppies and kittens are, they're also really messy and squirmy.

"Oh, and, Traci, Dave had a great idea," Amanda said. Dave is Traci's brother, and he and Amanda are seriously crushing on each other. "He thought we should post a sign-up sheet in the ward so that kids can choose what animal they'd like to play with. Also, that way, if anyone has any allergies, they can let us know."

Dave should know about allergies, I thought. Even though he's insanely allergic to animals, he decided to do Healing Paws with us last week to be around Amanda. He spent the entire day sneezing and blowing his nose. But I have to say he looked as happy as a clam, anyway.

"That's actually a good idea," Traci said. "Are you sure it came from Dave?" Then she shot an awkward glance at Amanda. I bet she realized that she'd just insulted the guy Amanda likes. It must be really weird to have your best friend like your annoying older brother.

But Amanda just smiled at Traci to show her she didn't mind.

"So what about the kids? Were they cute?" Felicia asked.

"Actually, yeah," Amanda said. "They were really cute. That little boy with the broken leg is so funny! He played with the gerbils, and he let one sit on top of his head the whole time we were there."

Felicia laughed the hardest. "I can't wait to see them again next weekend."

"You know, it really wasn't the same without you guys," Amanda said. "If we all aren't there, it just seems . . . kind of empty."

"I know what you mean," I said. "It felt like something was missing."

Just then Ryan came over with his lunch tray. He's been hanging around with us a lot lately. Actually, I'm pretty sure he and Traci are crushing on each other.

"Hey, Ryan, welcome back," Amanda said.

"Thanks. So, um, hey, is it all right if I eat with you guys?" He looked awkwardly at Traci, who seemed to be blushing. I looked from one to the other and back again. Ryan *never* ate lunch with us— he sat with a bunch of immature guys at a table across the room. There was only one reason why he would want to sit with a bunch of girls. Her name began with a *T* and ended with a *raci*.

"Sure, Ryan," Amanda said, looking over at them curiously. "Plop right down and have a seat."

Ryan looked down at Traci, who hadn't moved over for him to sit even though there was a lot more room on her side. Finally, she scooted over, and I noticed that she was bright red. What was going *on* here?

I made a mental note to give Traci a hard time about it later. I had always teased her about liking Ryan, but now I knew for sure.

"Congratulations on your award, Ryan," Amanda said.

He had won first place for playing the violin or something at the orchestra competition. I know nothing about music, but I guess he's supposed to be really good.

"Thanks," Ryan said, and I waited for him to make

a joke. He can never be serious for more than a few seconds. "It wasn't me, though. I hired a professional violinist to sit under the stage and play, and I just moved the bow like I was playing."

"Wow, you did a great job faking, Ryan," Felicia said, laughing. "You had us completely fooled."

And then, making the lunch a total love fest, Traci's brother, Dave, came over with his lunch tray.

"Hi, Dave!" Amanda said all happily. "Come over and sit down. I mean . . ." She shot a nervous glance at Traci. "I mean, if . . ."

Traci looked from Amanda to her brother. "Yeah, Dave, come sit down." She looked at Amanda and gave her a little smile. Amanda looked really grateful. But when Dave sat down next to Amanda, I saw Traci cross her eyes at him. Dave responded by sticking out his tongue for a split second while Amanda was concentrating on her sandwich.

"Mom says to meet her after school and she'll give us a ride home," Dave told Traci. Dave and Traci's mom, Ms. McClintic, is the new music teacher at our school. She's also my, Traci's, and Amanda's homeroom teacher. I guess she's pretty nice but awfully ditzy.

"Okay," Traci said. "Um, how was your history test?"

"Uh, it went quite well, actually. I was pleasantly surprised," he said.

Traci looked like she was trying to keep from laughing, and I knew why: "Quite well"? "Pleasantly surprised"? Dave *never* talked like that—he was obviously showing off for Amanda! I grinned, knowing that Traci was going to give him no end of grief for it later.

"Don't look now," Felicia said in a low voice, "but Arielle, I think you have an admirer at six . . . no, seven o'clock."

I turned right around, totally forgetting the "don't look now" part. Oops. I caught the eye of some tall guy who was looking right at me as he walked by. I'm used to this kind of thing, actually. I don't want to sound conceited, but I've turned a few heads in my day.

This guy wasn't my type, though, at *all*.

"He's walked by at least three times, trying to get your attention," Felicia said with a grin.

"Well, he can keep on walking. He's just a seventh grader," I said. "Plus, look at how skinny he is."

There was no way I was going to go out with any seventh-grade guy. Not at this stage of the game. There was no reason for me not to hold out for an eighth grader, and I had my eye on one in particular—Eric Rich. In fact, I was developing a foolproof plan to get Eric's attention as we spoke.

"I think that guy's name is Patrick," Felicia said, watching him walk away. "He plays on the basketball team. You don't think he's cute?" she asked. "I think he's totally cute."

I rolled my eyes. "Not at *all*, Felicia. He is *so* not my type. And besides, he's only a seventh grader," I added, finishing up my lunch.

"Arielle, what are you talking about?" Traci asked. "What do you mean, 'only a seventh grader'?"

"I've decided that if I'm going to like someone, it has to be an eighth grader or no one at all," I said.

Amanda shook her head at me. "Arielle, that's crazy. You mean to tell me that if you met someone you really liked who happened to be in seventh grade, you would reject him because he wasn't old enough for you?"

I shrugged. Easy for her to say since she'd already caught the eye of an eighth grader—Dave.

"Look, I don't *need* to settle for anything less than an eighth grader, so I won't. I want to hang out with popular seventh graders, too, but no seventh grader is going to be as popular as an eighth grader."

"All right, Arielle," Traci said, looking exasperated. "If that's what makes you happy. But I still think it's silly and a waste of perfectly good guys."

I shrugged again. I didn't really expect my friends to understand, anyway. Sometimes they seem really *young* when it comes to social issues like this. I'm kind of the leader in that department.

"I like your logic, Arielle," Dave said with a grin. "I'm glad to know that I'm a valuable commodity because I'm in eighth grade."

Traci rolled her eyes. "A valuable commodity?" He was *really* showing off for Amanda.

Amanda changed the subject. "I want to hear more about Chicago, you guys. Traci, you were so nervous about the clarinet part on that one song, remember? How did you do?"

"Oh, it went well, actually," Traci said. "I was *pleasantly surprised.*" She looked at me and winked.

"How did you finally manage to get comfortable with the song?" Amanda asked. But I knew this was a bad subject, so I kicked Amanda under the table to remind her.

Traci had met a guy from another school who helped her improve her clarinet playing, but the guy turned out to be a jerk who made everybody mad, especially Ryan.

Traci cast a nervous glance at Ryan, but he was studiously looking the other way.

"Oh, everybody helped me, but especially Ryan and Felicia. It was mostly a question of confidence. Once I realized how much my friends were behind me, I had no problem playing the piece."

Good save! I thought.

I knew she wanted to talk more about it and so did Felicia, but we couldn't in front of the guys.

Obviously, there was too much to talk about in just one lunch period. We had to get together after school.

"You guys, we have to have a little girl time, don't

you think?" I looked from Felicia to Amanda to Traci. "We have *so* much to catch up on."

Amanda nodded. "You're right. We have to spend some solid time together for sure."

"Yeah," Felicia agreed. "Why don't you guys come over to my house after school?"

"I can't—I have a dentist appointment," Amanda said sadly. "Unfortunately, I have a cavity that needs a filling."

"I can't, either," Traci said. "My mom and I are going shopping."

"I could come," I offered.

Felicia nodded. "That sounds great, but we should all try to get together soon. How about tomorrow?"

"No, Traci and I have soccer," I said. "What about Thursday?"

"Thursday's no good—we have an orchestra party to celebrate our awards," Traci said.

"Friday, then? At my house?" Felicia asked.

"Friday's good with me," Traci said.

"Yeah, me too," Amanda agreed.

"I know! What if we have a sleepover?" I suggested. "That way we have all night to talk."

"Oh, that sounds great!" Amanda cried.

"That would be awesome," Traci said excitedly. "We could make sundaes and give each other manicures. . . ."

"Okay, I'll ask my dad," Felicia said.

"We could call him right now," Amanda said, "on my

11

new cell phone! My dad thought I should have one for emergencies since I help baby-sit the twins so much."

"Oh, good idea. Let's try him," Felicia said.

Amanda took out her tiny red cell phone and pressed the microscopic buttons. She really loved having a cell phone, and she used it at every opportunity. I have to admit it was pretty cool. *Maybe I should ask my parents about getting one*, I thought.

She handed the phone over to Felicia when it started to ring.

"Hello?" Felicia suddenly looked annoyed. "Oh, hi, Penny, is my dad there?"

Penny was Felicia's dad's new girlfriend. They met because Penny was Amanda's baby-sitter, and while she was one of Amanda's all-time favorite people, Felicia wasn't too crazy about her. Neither was I, actually. I guess Penny's nice, but even though Felicia's parents have been divorced a few years, I think it was tough on her to see her dad with someone else.

"Hi, Dad," she said. "What's going on? . . . I was calling because I wanted to invite Traci and Amanda and Arielle to sleep over on Friday night. Is it okay? . . . Yes? . . . Thanks, I'll be home by four. Love you!"

"He said yes?" I asked.

"He did," she said.

"Okay, Friday it is, then. *Girls' night!*"

chapter
TWO

Instructions on henna box

Pour contents of packet number one into a large bowl. Add boiled water slowly in the ratio of one part water to three parts packet contents until mixture is a thick paste. Apply paste onto wet hair and let set for one hour. Without rinsing hair, apply contents of packet number two and let sit for one hour. Rinse hair with warm water. If product comes into contact with eyes, rinse thoroughly and contact a doctor.

Felicia and I hopped off the bus in front of her dad's house and ran down the long driveway. Behind her house is the Wonder Lake Animal Shelter. So there are animals wandering around all over the place, and there's a little barn for the cages. That afternoon, a couple of old horses were grazing in the fenced-in field next to the house, and the duck pond had geese and ducks in it.

"Oh, man. Penny is *still* here," Felicia complained as we rounded the corner of the driveway and saw Penny's car.

Speak of the devil—just then Penny came out of the house, waving and smiling. We both cringed.

"Hey, girls!" Mr. Fiol said, following Penny out of the house. Felicia's dad is kind of strict but also really nice.

"Hi, Mr. Fiol! Hi, Penny!" I called.

The only problem with hanging out at Felicia's house was that Mr. Fiol was always trying to get us to do work at the shelter even when it wasn't our day to volunteer.

"You girls look bored! How about cleaning out a few cages this afternoon?" he asked in a half-joking kind of way.

"Oh, Dad!" Felicia scowled at him. But then she hugged him, anyway.

"How was school today, girls?" Penny asked.

"It was great now that the orchestra is back and we're all together again," I told her.

Felicia just ignored the question.

"Honey, I have some bad news," Mr. Fiol said to Felicia.

"Oh, no. What is it?"

"Well, I just got a call from a horse farm in Michigan, and they have an old horse that they're going to have killed unless they find a place for it."

"Of course we'll take it. What's the trouble?" Felicia asked.

"I have to go there on Friday to pick up the horse, and I'll be gone overnight because it's such a long drive with the trailer. I guess you'll have to find another place for the sleepover."

"Oh." Felicia nodded. "Well, that's no problem, Dad. I'm sure we can have it at someone else's house," she said.

"Yeah, I'll ask my parents," I said.

"Wait, wait!" Penny looked from us to Mr. Fiol. "Um, you don't have to change your plans. I can stay here with the girls on Friday."

Felicia and I shared a Look. *Uh-oh. A sleepover with Penny?*

"You don't have to do that," Felicia said quickly.

"No, I want to! Really, I'd love to!" Penny insisted. "A sleepover! It sounds like so much fun."

"Are you sure, Penny? I don't want to put you out," Mr. Fiol said.

"Not at all. Is it okay with you, Felicia?" Penny asked.

I watched Felicia's face. I think she would rather eat nails than spend a night hanging out with all of her friends and Penny, but it wasn't like she could say that in front of her dad. And besides, Penny thought she was being nice. "Um, yeah, that sounds great. Thanks, Penny," Felicia said with a weak smile.

So there it was. Penny was going to be part of our sleepover, and there was no backing out now.

It would be too rude.

*   *   *

15

"Do mine in blue," Amanda said.

She fanned out her toenails, which I was about to paint. She had just painted mine in bright red, though I was going to have to do them over again because she messed up in a bunch of places.

But it doesn't matter, I reminded myself, *because this sleepover is about talking, not about having perfect feet. Besides, they're already pretty perfect.*

We were up in Felicia's room with the stereo turned up, playing Shauna Ferris—my favorite singer in the entire world. I'm probably her hugest fan. We were talking and doing each other's toes and generally catching up.

Felicia was clearly bummed that Penny was the one staying with us, but Penny was just downstairs by herself watching TV. She seemed to sense that we all wanted to be by ourselves. We had piled into Felicia's room and closed the door behind us.

After I was finished with Amanda's toes, I decided the time was right for Operation Get Traci to Admit She Likes Ryan.

"All right, Trace," I said, "it's time you came clean. I can't be the only person who's noticed that you seem to have a little something with someone we all know."

"What? Who? I don't know what you mean, Arielle," Traci lamely tried.

"I know what she's talking about, Traci," Amanda concurred. "You can try to play dumb, but you're not fooling us."

16

Traci looked helplessly at Felicia.

"Don't look at me," she said, laughing, "I was with you on the orchestra trip, so I saw you up close. You know you like him."

"Who?" Traci said, knowing she had lost and laughing about it.

"You tell us who," I said. "There's no reason for you not to say it. He so obviously likes you, too."

"You think?" Traci said, her face lighting up.

"*Aha!*" shouted Amanda. "So you admit that you like Ryan Bradley?"

"Yes, okay, okay, I admit it. I might like him a little," she said.

"Or you might like him a lot, from what I can see," I said. "But I'm not going to nitpick."

"Traci, anybody can tell that he likes you, too," Amanda said.

"Do you really, really think? How can you tell?" she asked.

"I've known him since we were little," Amanda told her, "and I've never seen him act this way before. He's always looking at you and coming up with excuses to hang around with you—"

"Totally. And Traci, do you remember how jealous he was of that guy Adam on the trip? He was acting crazy!" Felicia was talking about the guy who had helped Traci with the clarinet—the guy who'd turned out to be a jerk.

17

"Yeah, I guess so. Maybe you're right." Traci was beaming.

"Traci's got a booyyyfriend!" Amanda sang.

"Oh, look who's talking, Mrs. McClintic!" I said. We all laughed, then Traci made a funny face.

"Yeah, Amanda, maybe we could be sister-in-laws . . . or I guess it's sisters-in-law, right?" Traci said.

"That'd be great," Amanda said. "But seriously, Traci. It's a little weird that Dave is your brother. Does it bother you to have him hanging around with us all the time?"

"Well, at first it kind of freaked me out, but I'm getting used to it, and now it doesn't seem like a big deal. I just worry that you'll mind me making fun of him and teasing him. And I don't think he likes to be teased when you're around, so I have to stop myself all the time."

"I don't mind you teasing him. I think it's hilarious," she said. "The only thing that makes me feel funny is worrying that you're going to feel funny."

"That's what makes me uncomfortable, too. I don't really care if Dave is uncomfortable," Traci said, laughing. "After all, he's my annoying older brother."

"Then we're fine?" Amanda asked.

"Yeah, I think so. How about if we promise to tell each other right away if anything feels weird?"

"Okay, good idea. I promise," Amanda said.

"I promise, too," Traci said, and they shook hands.

"Well!" I said. "I'm so glad you two got all that off

your chests! Now can we please talk about ME? I have to tell you guys about who I like."

"You already told us, Arielle, remember?" Traci grinned and crossed her eyes. "Eric Rich, the *eighth* grader."

"Yes!" I cried. "But I want to tell you *all* about him. You know who he is, right? He's the guy with longish brown hair and blue eyes. He's on the track team. He does the high jump. It's amazing."

"Yeah, I know him. He's friends with Dave," Traci said. "I think he was even over at our house once."

"So obviously he's really athletic, but he's also really smart. He writes for the newspaper, did you know? He's the one who wrote that story last year about how the meat they were serving us for hot lunch wasn't food grade. He actually sneaked into the food storage room at school and looked on the boxes. They said, 'Not fit for human consumption.'"

"I heard about that from my mother," Traci said. "The head of the school lunch program got fired over it."

"Exactly! So you see why I like him so much," I said.

"That and because he's in eighth grade." Amanda rolled her eyes.

"That's right," I said proudly. They could make fun of me all they wanted, but if being popular was important to me, who were they to knock it?

"Hey, can anybody French-braid?" Traci asked, probably to avoid all of us getting into an argument about the eighth-grader question.

"I can!" Amanda said. "Want me to braid your hair?"

"Yeah," Traci said. She had really thick, long blond hair. It would look great if she blow-dried it, but she never did. She usually just wore it pulled back in a ponytail. But she was so pretty, it didn't really matter how her hair looked.

Amanda started braiding Traci's hair in two braids, one on each side, and Felicia sat on her bed. Actually, she looked kind of sad, eating one chocolate chip cookie after another.

"So let me tell you guys my plan to get Eric to notice me," I said.

"You have a plan?" Traci asked.

"Yes, definitely. And it's foolproof," I told them. "You know how there's a fall chorus concert in three weeks?"

Traci laughed. "Know about it? It's my entire life at home. My mother doesn't talk about anything else, and she made me walk around the school putting up posters for *two hours* the other day."

Ms. McClintic was in charge of the concert because she's the music director of the school.

"But what about it, Ari? How is that going to get Eric's attention?" Felicia asked. It was about the first thing she'd said all night.

"Well, one of the numbers is a Shauna solo!" I said.

"I know." Traci nodded. "My mom wanted to put a song by a popular singer in the program, and she asked me who she should pick. Would you believe she'd never even *heard* of Shauna Ferris? What planet does she live on?" Traci asked.

"Well, I dunno. But listen: I'm going to sing that song in the show!" I looked at my friends eagerly. "And the whole school is going to see it, and I'm going to be so amazing that Eric Rich is going to fall in love with me!"

Everyone just looked at me.

All right, I thought, *I should have known they wouldn't be able to understand what I was talking about.*

"Arielle, don't you have to audition and get the song first?" Traci asked.

I shrugged. "I don't think anyone else is going to try out for it but me. Everyone knows I want it."

What I didn't tell them, but was pretty sure of, was that no one else from chorus would dare try out for it since they knew I wanted it. I was the most popular person who would try out for this concert at all, and no one else stood a chance against me.

"Well, let's say you do get the part . . . do you even know how to sing?" Amanda asked.

"Is there anyone on the *planet* who knows Shauna's music better than me?" I asked them.

"Well, no, probably not," Traci said. "But you have to sing it by yourself. You're used to just singing along."

"Listen," I told them, "I'm going to get up there onstage, dressed in an outfit that Shauna herself would kill for, and I'm going to dance just like her and sing the song, and I'm going to be the star of Wonder Lake Middle School. And if you doubt me . . . just wait and see. I'll have Eric Rich eating out of the palm of my hand when this is over."

"Okay, Arielle, if you say so," Amanda said, looking like she wasn't so sure.

Well, I was.

"Hey, Felicia, do you want to have a bed-jumping demonstration?" Traci asked her. Felicia was still just sitting on her bed, eating cookies.

"What's that?" I asked.

"When we were in the hotel in Chicago, Felicia and I made up a dance to do while we jumped on the beds. We were pretty good except Felicia kept falling between the bed and the wall and getting stuck!"

We all laughed, and Traci jumped up on Felicia's bed and started jumping all around her. Felicia smiled a little, but she didn't look like she meant it.

"You seem like you're still pretty bummed, Felicia. Is it because of Penny?" Amanda asked in a low voice so Penny wouldn't overhear.

Felicia frowned and sighed. "Yeah. I'm sorry, you guys. It just really bothers me to have her here, like she's my mom or something. And I wanted this to be such a fun night. I hope I'm not ruining it for all of you," she said.

"No way! I'm having a blast," Traci said.

"Yeah, me too," I said. "I'm just sad because you're

not having fun. We need to come up with a plan to cheer you up."

"Good idea. How about we make crank calls to boys?" Amanda suggested.

"No. I don't really feel like it." Felicia sighed again.

"Okay, then, do you want us to give you a facial?" Traci asked.

"Um, not really. Sorry," Felicia said.

"Wait a minute! Hang on." I'd had a major brainstorm. I got up on the bed because I was so excited.

"Listen to this. I have the ultimate plan to cheer up Felicia," I said. Everybody just looked up at me.

"We are going to give Felicia . . . a *makeover!*"

Traci and Amanda cheered.

"Great idea!" Traci shouted.

Felicia shook her head. "You guys. I'm really not in the mood to be the center of attention. Can't we just play a game of crazy eights or something?"

"No way!" I said. "Do you have any idea what kind of an offer this is? Not many people get to be made over by the world's foremost professional in makeovers."

"She's right, Felicia," Amanda said. "Nobody knows about fashion and grooming like Arielle. This is not something you want to pass up."

"I can guarantee you that you are going to look much, *much* different when all this is over," I told her. "Heck, you may even end up looking as good as me!"

"I guess it does kinda sound like fun," Felicia said, smiling a little.

"It's not fun. It's serious business!" I said, joking around. "What could be more important than looking good?"

"I know she's kidding," Traci put in, "but you know what they say, 'When you feel good about how you look, then you feel better in general.'"

"Absolutely right," I agreed. "Now we need to gather our supplies."

"Okay. What do we need?" Felicia asked, looking a little happier.

"Well, let's see . . . Traci, you go and get the blow-dryer and hair spray from the bathroom. Amanda, you're in charge of manicure and pedicure materials. We need a file, and a buffer, and all the nail polish we can find—we have to get the color right. Also, we need a few towels and some makeup remover so we can try different looks."

"Okay!" Traci said, and she and Amanda ran off to find everything.

"Felicia, you should go and take a quick shower so your hair's clean, and I'll get all my makeup together from my overnight bag. Luckily, I have a ton of stuff with me."

"All right," Felicia said, "here I go."

As she started to walk out of the room, though, Penny came through the door with a big goofy smile.

"Hey, girls! What's all the commotion? Are you up to something good?"

Penny had on what could only be called a smock. It was a kind of loose dress that came down to just below her knees—a very awkward length. She wore her hair in a long braid down her back, and even though she has a really pretty face, she looked like she had stepped straight out of the 1970s.

Really, the only good thing she had going on was a really beautiful wire necklace and earrings set that must have been handmade.

"A makeover!" she said when we told her what we were doing. "Can I help? I *love* makeovers!"

She said she had some great makeup and ran to get her purse.

"Are you okay?" I asked Felicia when Penny was out of earshot.

"Yeah, I guess so," she said. "I mean, I have to just deal with this, I guess." She looked after Penny with a frown.

Penny ran back up the stairs with her purse in hand.

"Okay, here it is," she said, taking a beat-up-looking makeup case from her bag. She opened it and took out blush, some lip gloss, and some eye shadow, all in some no-name organic brand.

"That looks great," I lied. "We can sure use the extra colors."

Then I had a brainstorm.

"But, Penny, you know what you could maybe do

that would be so, so great?" I asked in my nicest voice.

"What? Anything, you name it," she said. I was beginning to feel bad for thinking such mean things about her. She really was a nice person.

"Well, we wanted to henna Felicia's hair, but we'd have to go to the drugstore to get the henna. I wondered if . . . maybe . . ."

"You want me to pick some up? I'd be happy to run to the drugstore. Just write down exactly what you need so I don't get the wrong thing."

"Thanks, Penny," Felicia said. "That's really sweet of you."

She sounded like she meant it.

See? The makeover plan was working already.

chapter
THREE

Note on Felicia's mirror from Arielle

ARIELLE DAVIS'S SECRET FORMULA FOR
PROPER PRESENTATION

1. Look GREAT, all the time. DON'T even go to get the mail looking undone.
2. Walk tall with your shoulders back and your head up. Imagine that you're trying to touch your elbows behind your back.
3. SMILE at boys, but then look away.
4. PROJECT CONFIDENCE—pretend you're comfortable even if you're nervous. "Fake it till you make it."

With Penny gone and out of the way, we decided to get to work.

After she got out of the shower, I sat Felicia down in front of the mirror and we all took a long look.

"Now, Felicia, I want you to be prepared," I told

her. "A makeover can be kind of strange because you don't recognize yourself afterward."

"She's right," Amanda said. "She gave me a makeover once, and every time I looked in the mirror, I got completely confused."

"Okay," Felicia said.

"There are four different parts to the makeover process," I explained. "They are: one, hair; two, makeup; three, clothes; and four, most important, presentation."

"Presentation?" Felicia asked.

"Yes. Let me explain," I continued. "The first three, hair, clothes, and makeup, we'll do together. The last, presentation, is all about attitude. It may take some more time and coaching."

"Okay, Arielle, you're the expert," Felicia said. She looked a little nervous, I thought, but that was okay. At least she didn't look sad anymore.

"Should we get started on makeup while we wait for Penny to get back with the henna?" Amanda asked.

"Yeah, good idea," I said.

We had Felicia sit down in a chair with a towel around her neck, and Traci and Amanda helped me spread out all the makeup on the bed next to me. I had an idea of what I wanted to do, but I wanted to be able to try out different things, so we had makeup remover and cotton balls on hand.

I sat down on a chair in front of Felicia.

"Okay, Feleesh. I'm going to start with the basics. This is a little light foundation," I told her as I applied it with a sponge. "You don't even really need it because your skin is perfect, but it makes a nice base for the other makeup. You probably won't want to wear it every day."

"Okay," Felicia said. She sat with her eyes closed, facing away from the mirror.

"Now I'm going to put on some blush to bring out your cheekbones. You have great cheekbones," I said.

"She does," Traci agreed.

I was glad that Traci and Amanda were letting me run the show. They didn't even really wear makeup, so I guess it made sense that I would be in charge.

"Okay, now we're going to do your eyes. The eyes are the absolute most important part of the makeup. That's what draws people to your face."

I started with eyeliner in a brown that matched Felicia's eyelashes so it looked really natural. In my opinion, there's nothing worse looking than too much of the wrong shade of eyeliner.

"That looks great, Arielle," Traci said.

"You think? Pass me a Q-tip, would you—I was just thinking I'd try a little lighter on the upper lid."

I fiddled with Felicia's eyeliner until it was perfect and then took a step back to admire my work.

"Okay. Now we're getting somewhere," I said.

"Felicia, you look amazing so far," Amanda told her.

"Let me look. I want to see," she said, trying to turn toward the mirror.

"No way," Traci said, grabbing her and laughing. "You have to see it all at once. Otherwise it's no fun. It'll be worth the wait."

"All right." Felicia was giggling now. *Hooray*, I thought. Finally she was cheering up.

"Okay, now I'm going to put a little eye shadow and mascara on you, and then all that's left is the lips."

I tried a couple of different looks with the shadow and finally settled on a really natural bronze on her upper lid, with a little bit of darker brown on the crease. Everything looked very natural.

"Wow, Arielle. You really know what you're doing," Amanda noted.

"Yes, I do. Now, do you think we go with darker shades for the lips or stick to the natural theme?"

"Maybe something darker. It's sexier," Traci said.

I let Traci pick out a pretty coral color and carefully applied liner to Felicia's lips, followed by the lipstick.

"Okay, Felicia, we're just about done. Let me just look you over and then you can see."

"I'm nervous," she said.

"You should be—you look so good, you're going to have a heart attack," Amanda said.

She was right. It was incredible how good Felicia looked. She was naturally really pretty, but the makeup enhanced her looks and made her absolutely gorgeous.

"Okay. We're done. Are you ready?" I asked her.

"I guess so," she said.

She closed her eyes and turned around to face the mirror.

"Here goes. On three, I'm going to open my eyes. One . . . two . . . *three*." Felicia opened her eyes and stared at herself in the mirror, looking stunned. "I don't *believe* it! Look at me!"

"I know!" Traci said with a giggle. "You're amazing."

Felicia just stared at herself for about thirty seconds. Then she looked at her profile, then straight on.

"I don't believe it," she said finally. "I never imagined I could look like this."

Just then Penny called from downstairs, "I'm back! Are you gorgeous yet?"

We could hear her running up the stairs, then she entered the room and stopped short when she saw Felicia.

"Holy *cow*," she said. "You look like a model, Felicia."

"You think?" Felicia asked. She looked back to the mirror.

"Yes, I do. I mean, you look so incredible, I can't believe it," Penny said. "Walk into any modeling agency, and I bet you'd get a contract."

"My dad would never let me leave the house with makeup on, though," Felicia said, suddenly looking bummed.

Penny smiled. "Don't worry, hon, I can talk him into it," she said with a wink at Felicia.

Felicia had kind of a funny look on her face. I could see that she was perfectly torn between being psyched that she would be able to wear makeup and being bummed because Penny had so much say in her dad's opinions.

"Well, anyway, here's the henna," Penny said, taking it out of the bag and handing it to me.

"Okay, let's get this in your hair, Felicia. It's going to have to set for a while, and we can get started on clothes while it's in."

Felicia looked at the henna box uncertainly. "Do you think my dad will be mad that I dyed my hair?"

"Oh, that's the great thing about henna, sweetie." Penny patted Felicia's shoulder gently. "It's completely natural, and it washes out in a few shampoos."

I nodded. "It won't completely change your hair color, Feleesh. It'll just add some nice red highlights. You'll probably want to do it in the sink, and be careful not to wash off your makeup."

Felicia looked from Penny to me and smiled. "All right, guys." She turned and walked into the bathroom. "Here goes nothing."

I went into Felicia's closet while Traci and Amanda and Penny helped Felicia with the henna.

Felicia had a lot of really nice quality things but not much that was exciting. I managed to find a couple of things that would get some attention if she wore them together. I set the clothes aside and went to check out the progress on the henna.

"Do you girls want to get a pizza and have dinner while we wait for the henna to set?" Penny asked.

"Yeah!" we all said in a chorus.

"I think we look at your hair in only about ten more minutes," I said, taking a swig of soda. We were sitting at the kitchen table, the remains of a large veggie pizza in front of us.

"I can't believe I'm going to be a redhead," Felicia said.

Traci grinned. "You're going to look so gorgeous!"

"I don't know." Felicia shook her head. "This might all be getting to be a little too much. I mean, I don't want to look *too* different, do I?"

"Why not?" I asked her. "Maybe with a new look you could have a whole new life."

"I like the life I have right now," she said, smiling. "But I guess I could stand to make a few changes. It would be nice if boys noticed me more, for one thing."

"At this rate you'll have to beat them off with a stick!" Penny said.

Felicia was in a bathrobe with her head wrapped in a blue towel. With her makeup on, she looked like a movie star in her dressing room. I had done a pretty darn good job, if I did say so myself.

"Are you ready for step two, you guys?" I asked, looking at my watch. "Because it's time to see what Felicia's new hair looks like."

We all ran up the stairs and Felicia sat down in front of the mirror again, and she got geared up to take the towel off her hair.

"Okay, Feleesh," I said. "It's wet now, so you probably won't be able to see much of a difference until we dry it. I'm going to put some styling lotion in your hair, and then we'll blow-dry it straight. Ready?"

Felicia nodded eagerly. "Let's go."

I whipped off the towel and got to work. We rinsed out Felicia's hair with warm water, then I put in some styling lotion and pulled out the blow-dryer.

"Ouch!" Felicia complained as I wound her hair around a big brush. "That hurts!"

"I know, honey," I said. "Beauty can be so painful."

As her hair started to dry, though, I could see Traci and Amanda's expressions begin to change. "Wow," Amanda mouthed to me over Felicia's head. "I know," I mouthed back. When her hair was done, it was straight and as glossy as a mirror. It swished around her face and just looked amazing. "Are you ready, Felicia?" I asked as I made one last circle with the blow-dryer. "It looks pretty dry. Ready to see your new color?"

Felicia looked up at me and nodded. "Definitely."

I turned her around to face the mirror, and Felicia's face broke into a huge grin. "Oh, my God. It's so straight! I love it!"

"What a great color!" Amanda said.

"It looks beautiful," Penny said in an awed voice.

"Arielle, you are incredible. Look at her hair! It looks like she just came from the salon!" Amanda said. "Where did you learn how to do that?"

"Well, I do it myself to my own hair every single morning, so I've had a lot of practice."

The thing was, Felicia's hair did look better than mine. She had thicker hair, and the color really suited her. I felt a little itch of jealousy, but I made myself be a good friend and ignore it.

Felicia was just staring at herself in the mirror, amazed and obviously very happy. Penny was hovering around her, and for once Felicia looked like she didn't mind a bit.

"Okay, now for step three: clothes," I announced. "Felicia, I already looked at your stuff and found an outfit for you."

I opened the closet door and took out the stuff I had chosen and handed it to her on a hanger.

She looked appalled. "Arielle, I could never wear this top with this skirt. The colors are so bright. I'll look ridiculous if I wear them together."

"Just trust me, will you?" I said, getting a pair of boots out of the closet.

"And THOSE boots with this? No way. You'd have to be crazy."

"Just try it on and you'll see," I said. "I'm *never* wrong about clothes."

"That's true, actually. She's never wrong about clothes," Amanda told her.

"Okay, I'll try it, but you have to promise not to laugh," Felicia said.

She put on the sweater I gave her. It was a gorgeous royal blue, perfect for the purple miniskirt I'd picked out. Actually, I didn't think I had ever seen Felicia wear that miniskirt.

Felicia deliberately didn't look in the mirror as she got dressed. She zipped up the boots, which were almost knee-high, and turned her back to the mirror.

I had to smile when she stood up in the outfit. She looked amazing. There was no denying it. She actually looked as good if not better than me on a *good* day. I felt a twinge of jealousy again but managed to ignore it.

"Oh, my gosh," Traci said.

"Wowee," Amanda said.

"I can't believe it," Penny echoed.

"What, you guys? Do I look ridiculous?" Felicia asked.

"No. Just the opposite. Turn around and look in the mirror," I said.

She slowly turned around and looked. A huge smile appeared on her face.

"Wow. I *do* look good," she whispered.

She did, too. She was completely transformed. I had never seen anything like it. She looked like she ought to be in a movie or a magazine. I had done a good job. *Too bad I can't get school credit for this*, I thought.

"Wait one second," Penny said, and took out her beautiful wire earrings and handed them to Felicia. Felicia put them on, and Penny took off her wire necklace and fastened it around Felicia's neck. The dark purple stone fell perfectly in the hollow of her throat. It looked exactly right.

"Beautiful," Penny said.

"Thanks, Penny," Felicia murmured, looking at herself in the mirror.

"You have to go to school like this on Monday," Traci said.

"Oh, I could *never* leave the house like this. I'd be so embarrassed!" she said.

"Embarrassed?" I asked. "You should be proud. Walk tall. You are definitely going to school like this on Monday."

"My dad would never let me, anyway," she objected.

"No, I told you. I'll take care of that," Penny said.

"You think you really could convince him?" Felicia asked.

"For sure, hon. I know I could." Penny smiled. "I'd be happy to."

"Well . . ." Felicia scrunched up her face, considering.

37

"I don't know. I guess I could try it," she said. "I mean, one day couldn't hurt, right?"

"We'll stay close to keep the photographers away," Amanda joked.

"Now, I'm going to write out the rules of presentation for you to keep posted by your mirror," I told her. "The last step of the makeover is for you to read them and try your best to follow them. Attitude is everything!"

"Thanks, Arielle," Felicia said, and walked over to give me a big hug. "I don't know what to say. I could never look this way without your help."

"Aw, come on, Feleesh," I said, feeling awkward. "It's no big thing. It's what I do." Felicia pulled away and looked in the mirror again. I grinned at Traci and Amanda and then went to look for a pen.

chapter
FOUR

Written on the top of the page of a book by the captain of the football team to his friend during second-period English with Mr. Fromme

Did you see that new girl? She's smokin'.

She isn't new. That's that girl Felicia. She just looks totally different. . . .

Wow, you can say that again, dude.

"So I just pull it straight with the brush and then aim the blow-dryer at it until it's dry?" Felicia asked me over the phone on Sunday night.

"Right, but you have to keep doing it over and over again from different angles," I said.

"But don't your arms get tired?" she asked.

"Totally, they do. But it's like an upper-body workout every morning," I said. Felicia laughed, but I was serious.

"How long do you think it will take me? It took

you forty-five minutes to dry my hair," she said.

"Yeah, I would give yourself at least an hour," I said. I spend at least an hour on my hair every morning. But it's totally worth it as far as I'm concerned.

"An hour! I'm going to have to get up at dawn," she complained.

"Also give yourself plenty of time for makeup. You want to go slow to get it right and be able to fix any mistakes you make. Just remember: Don't overdo. Less is more when it comes to makeup."

"Okay, Arielle. I may have to call you at five tomorrow morning if I get flustered," she said.

"Great," I joked back. "You can tell my answering machine all about it."

"I think my dad is going to have a cow when he sees me in the morning with all this makeup on."

"Didn't Penny talk to him?" I asked.

"Yeah, she did, but I don't think he knows *how* different I'm going to look."

"Well, just remind him that he gave you permission, so he can't take it back now," I said.

"But what if he says I can't leave the house looking like I'm going to?"

"Then tell him you're going to tell Penny!"

We both laughed.

"Okay, so I'll see you tomorrow?" I said.

"Will you meet me at the bike racks so we can walk in together?" she asked me. "I'm totally nervous."

"Yeah, of course. I'll see you there at eight-forty so we'll have a couple of minutes to get prepared," I said.

"Good idea, but I don't know if I'll ever be prepared for this," she said.

"You'll do fine, Felicia. I just know it," I reassured her. "What's the worst that could happen?"

"Well . . . I guess you're right," she said. "I'll see you in the morning."

"Hey, Traci!" I called, seeing her pull up to the front door of the school in her mom's minivan. "Hey, Ms. McClintic, see you in class," I called.

Ms. McClintic waved, and Traci came running up.

"I'm waiting for Felicia," I told her. "She's late."

"Do you think she'll really go through with it? Her new look, I mean?"

"Yeah, she called me for advice about her hair last night, so . . ."

"Hey! There she is. Felicia!" Traci called. Felicia was rushing from the bus stop, and she looked gorgeous in her outfit and hair and makeup. Her presentation, however, was completely lame.

We only had a few minutes, so I was going to have to work fast.

"Hey, Felicia. You look perfect. You got your makeup and your hair just right," I said.

"You think? Thanks. I did the thing you said ab—"

"Sorry, but I have to interrupt because we only have five minutes before class."

"What do you mean?" she asked. "What is it?"

"We have to do a crash course on presentation. You're walking like you're embarrassed, and that just will *not* do. Let me see you stand up straight."

She did immediately.

"Okay, now. Don't look down at the ground or at your feet. Look straight ahead, and if you don't want to look at someone when you pass, don't look down, look behind them. Always keep your eyes up."

"Okay," she said, "got it."

"Now, and this is the most important, you have to make sure you don't frown or look unhappy. You don't want people to think you're snobby."

"So what do I do?" she asked.

"Imagine that you're in a good mood even if you're not. Put a little smile on your face like you're a pleasant person, but make sure you don't smile like an idiot."

She tried it. Head up, shoulders back, smiling contentedly. It worked.

"Wow. Big difference," Traci said. "I'll have to try this."

"Great," I told Felicia. "Now you look comfortable and happy."

"I'm really not," she said with her pleasant smile.

"That doesn't matter. What matters is how people think you feel, not how you actually feel," I said.

"Arielle, you realize that sounds completely ridiculous," Traci said. "You look great, Felicia. Just be yourself as much as you can."

"Don't listen to her," I said, "unless you want to grow up to be a childless old maid."

We all laughed but got interrupted by the bell.

As we rushed inside to make it to class on time, I noticed that Felicia was drawing looks from everyone. Everyone was staring as we walked down the hall. I had no illusions about the fact that today they were not staring at me. They were staring at Felicia.

She barely looked like herself, actually, and probably some people thought she was a new person at the school.

"Check it out, Felicia! All the guys are looking at you like they don't know what hit them," Traci said.

"No, they're looking at Arielle, as usual," she said.

"No, they're not. They're looking at you," I said. "Believe me, I think I know the difference."

It was the slightest bit annoying, actually, to see all those guys looking at Felicia.

"Hey, there's Amanda," Traci said.

"Wow! Look at you," she said to Felicia, who tried on her pleasant smile again.

"Hey, Amanda. What do you think? Can I pull this off today?"

"Totally, girl. You look amazing," Amanda said.

We headed to the hallway where our lockers were. Felicia grabbed my arm and said, "Come with me to my locker. I don't want to go by myself."

"But it's just right over there," I said.

"Please! Just come with me," she pleaded.

"Oh, all right."

We went to her locker, and still, everyone who passed by was checking her out.

"So as I was leaving the house, I went to say good-bye to my dad, and he told me to go back up to my room and change and take off some of my makeup," she said.

"No way!" I said. "So what did you do?"

"Well, I went back up to my room, but instead of doing what he said, I called Penny."

"You didn't!" I said, laughing.

"Yes. And she said for me to bring the phone downstairs to him and she would talk to him. So I went down and handed him the phone, and she talked him out of stopping me."

"What did he say?" I asked, amazed.

"He was saying, 'I would never have agreed if I had known she was going to be dressed like a movie star!'"

"And then what?" I asked. This was too funny.

"Then he hung up the phone and said he was sorry and told me to have a great day at school," she said.

"Go, Penny! I can't believe that!" I said.

"I know." She laughed.

Then I noticed a group of eighth-grade girls standing nearby, looking over at us and talking.

After a few seconds they walked right over.

"Hi!" I said to them.

"Hey," one of them said back, but then they ignored me and turned to Felicia.

"Hey," Felicia said, doing a great job of smiling and standing up straight.

"Hi, there! We were just noticing how great you look. The outfit is fabulous."

"And I love your hair," one of the girls said with a smile.

"Thank you so much. That's really nice of you," Felicia said. She handled it very well.

As they walked away, it kind of bugged me a little bit. Felicia could have mentioned that I was the one who had given her the makeover. I mean, I did all the work, and she was getting all the credit. It wasn't really fair, I thought.

But then I stopped myself again. What was wrong with me? I promised myself I would be a good friend, and that meant letting Felicia have her moment in the sun.

I went to my locker for a minute, and the four of us walked in the direction of our classrooms.

"Oh my God, do you see that guy looking at you, Felicia?" Amanda asked her. "He's practically drooling on the floor!"

"HI!" a really cute seventh grader said to Felicia as we passed.

"Wow," she said after he'd walked by. "This is weird."

Then I saw Eric Rich coming down the hall.

I stood up straighter and smiled in preparation. Then I remembered who I was standing next to.

Oh, no, I thought. *If he notices her and not me, I'll die.*

But as he passed us, sure enough, he and his friends looked straight at Felicia and then turned to each other and started whispering. Worse, I watched as he walked away and he turned back around to look at her again on his way down the hall.

For a second my blood boiled. It was one thing to have other people looking at her. But Eric Rich was a different matter entirely.

Before I knew it, I was saying something mean to Felicia.

"Ohhh," I said sympathetically, "Felicia, your hair is starting to frizz up on the ends. You have to let me show you how to dry it properly so that doesn't happen."

"What are you talking about, Arielle?" Traci asked. "Her hair is perfect."

"It really is, Felicia," Amanda said. "I think Arielle is just trying to psych you out."

"Be quiet, Amanda, I am not," I said. But I didn't push the issue because she was right.

Felicia brought her hand up to her hair worriedly, and I felt a moment of satisfaction.

Since me, Traci, and Amanda were in the same homeroom, we had to split off from Felicia as she went to her own homeroom.

We stood in the hall for a minute, talking before she had to leave, and I could not believe the kind of attention Felicia was getting. People were walking by and doing double takes and then turning to their friends to whisper about her.

I noticed a lot of older guys were looking her way, too, and that gave me another pang of jealousy. I made myself ignore it. It was fine for Felicia to have some moments of her own, I told myself. It was important to be a good friend.

"Okay," I said to her. "You look great. Just remember these three rules: smile, stand up straight, look up."

"I got it," she said as she brought her finger up to her mouth to chew her nail.

I grabbed her arm. "And *no* biting your fingernails!"

"Oh, yeah," she said. "Sorry. Okay. See you guys at lunch. But will you meet me outside the lunchroom? I'm scared to go in by myself."

"Okay," I agreed, even though I was already dreading the reaction she was going to get in the lunchroom.

"See you later, Felicia," Traci said.

"Be careful out there," Amanda said, and Felicia laughed and waved good-bye.

We kept walking down the hall toward our classroom.

"Can you believe all these guys looking at her?" Amanda said. "Maybe you can do a makeover on me next time." She laughed.

"Oh, they'll get sick of her in no time," I said grouchily. "Guys are just interested in whatever's the next new thing."

"Arielle, that's not very nice. You should just be happy for her and try not to get so jealous," Traci said.

"Who's jealous? I'm not jealous. I'm just saying that people are really fickle," I said.

"Well, be careful not to be fickle yourself, honey," Amanda said.

"What's that supposed to mean?" I demanded.

"Just be nice to Felicia. This is going to be weird for her, and she needs our help and support," Amanda said.

"Oh, all right," I said. I knew that's what I had to do.

chapter
FIVE

Felicia's morning

5:30–5:43	shower
5:43–6:28	blow-dry hair
6:28–7:05	apply makeup
7:05–7:07	remove makeup and start again
7:07–7:42	reapply makeup
7:42–8:05	get dressed
8:05–8:10	eat breakfast
8:10	leave for school

When I got into math class, my last class before lunch, and sat down, three boys were having a loud conversation near the front.

"No, dude, I'm telling you it's that girl Felicia. I know her from band," one guy said.

"No way that's her—how could she look so totally different?" another one said.

"I don't know, but she does."

"*Yeah*, she does. She's definitely the hottest girl in the whole school."

"Dude, she's the hottest girl I've ever *seen*."

I rolled my eyes, opened my book, and tried to look over the homework I had done last night. *Where* was Mr. Reid? I never thought I'd actually be glad to see him. But if I had to listen to that conversation about Felicia any longer, I would go insane.

Finally Mr. Reid came in.

"Class, please take out your homework. . . ."

Ahhh, I thought, *music to my ears*.

I found myself walking kind of slowly through the halls to the cafeteria because I wasn't really looking forward to lunch. Normally I really like lunch. I like to see who's around, and occasionally, I catch a glimpse of Eric Rich on his way out to the eighth graders' lounge.

Today, though, I knew it would be all about Felicia and her amazing new look. I promised myself that I would try to be generous about the whole thing. After all, it was my idea to do the makeover in the first place.

I couldn't exactly get mad at Felicia just because I did too good of a job.

"Hey, Arielle," she said with a big smile as I walked up. "Boy, am I glad to see you."

"Hey, Felicia, how's it been going?" I asked.

"Well, three boys asked me for my phone number, and Mr. Korstange didn't recognize me. He thought I was a foreign exchange student."

"He did? What country did he think you were from?" I asked her, laughing.

Traci and Amanda came walking up.

"You know, I would never recognize you if I ran into you on the street," Amanda told Felicia.

"Do you have an agent yet?" Traci asked her with a grin.

"No, but I'm starting to really enjoy this, actually. Are you guys ready to go in?" she asked.

I braced myself as we walked through the lunchroom door. Sure enough, two separate conversations stopped as we walked by and I saw three girls whispering and pointing at Felicia.

"Well, it isn't letting up, is it?" Traci said to Felicia.

"No, but I feel like they're all just laughing at me for wearing these boots with this skirt," she joked. Obviously she knew they were all looking at her because she looked so good.

I was kind of annoyed that she would make a joke about the outfit I had picked out. I mean, clearly it was working.

"You should be lucky enough to have me pick out your clothes every day, Felicia. I didn't see you getting a whole lot of attention before I told you what to wear," I said, and immediately regretted it.

"Arielle! Felicia was just making a joke," Traci reprimanded me.

"Well, I know that," I said quickly.

51

Felicia didn't seem to notice that I had been rude to her. She was totally walking on air.

We made our way to our table by the window, and I took out my lunch of vegetable sushi. I watched Felicia walk across the lunchroom to the hot lunch line, and all the eyes following her, and the whispering that went on once she passed.

"She seems to be getting the hang of it," said Traci, who had also brought her lunch to school. She munched on her carrot sticks and watched Felicia.

"Yeah, I guess she's doing pretty well. She doesn't look as nervous as she did this morning," I said, trying to sound nice. "And look," I went on, "she's standing up straight, with her eyes up. She looks great."

Just then, as Felicia waited in the lunch line, I saw Serena Whitmore approach her. Serena Whitmore is the most popular seventh grader and one of the most popular girls in the whole school.

"Oh, my God, look," I said. "Serena Whitmore is talking to Felicia."

She and Felicia talked for a minute, and Felicia kept smiling and nodding. Then Serena pointed to a table across the lunchroom where she and her friends always sat. I knew because I had sat with them myself a bunch of times. Serena was kind of my friend.

Serena walked away with a wave, and Felicia went through the lunch line.

After a few minutes she came back with her tray, looking excited.

"Hey, you guys, listen. Serena Whitmore just asked me to sit at her table. She said she wanted to hear all about my makeover."

I had to stop myself from rolling my eyes.

"But I asked her if you could sit with them, too, Arielle, because I know you're friends," she said. "And besides, you're the one who should be talking about the makeover since you're the one who did it."

"Oh, you did?" I was so relieved. "That is so nice of you," I said, gathering up my lunch.

"Sorry, you guys," she said to Traci and Amanda. "I didn't want to ask her if three people could sit at their table. It seemed like it would be too much."

"No way! Don't apologize. I'm so psyched for you," Traci said.

"Me too. No worries, Felicia. It's cool," Amanda said.

"Okay, then. We'll see you at the lockers after last period," I said to them.

I saw that there wasn't much room at the table as we approached, and I quickly tried to figure out where I was going to sit. Serena had saved Felicia a seat, but it looked like I was on my own.

We walked up to Serena, and she moved aside so Felicia could sit down.

"Oh, no! I'm so sorry, Arielle," Serena said to me.

"So many people sat down after I went up to the lunch line. Do you promise you'll sit with us tomorrow? I'll definitely save you a seat."

"Oh, totally, it's no problem," I said, putting a pleasant smile on my face. Felicia gave me an apologetic look as I walked away, and I smiled at her, too.

But I was in a really bad mood as I walked back to our table.

"What happened?" Amanda asked me.

"No room," I said gruffly.

"Oh, well. It's amazing for Felicia that she gets a chance to sit with them," Traci said. "This is so cool."

"Yeah, maybe we'll get to start sitting with them, too," Amanda said.

"I already did start sitting with them, remember?" I shot testily. "I hope Felicia doesn't think she's their new best friend or something. I've known those girls since the beginning of the year."

"Arielle, what is *wrong* with you?" Amanda said. "You should be happy for Felicia that she gets to sit with the popular seventh graders. Like you said, you're already friends with them, so what do you care? Besides, this whole thing was your idea, remember?"

I knew she was right, and I should try to be more reasonable.

I couldn't help it, though. This whole Felicia-as-popular thing was really starting to get under my skin.

Dave came over and plopped his lunch down next

to Amanda. "What did you guys do to Felicia?" he asked us. "She looks nothing like her former self."

But before we could answer, Ryan arrived.

"Felicia's taken Wonder Lake by storm," he said. "It's kind of scary. Guys I've never talked to are asking me if I know her and if I can introduce them. And I saw an *Access Hollywood* van pull up out front."

"I know," Amanda said. "Can you believe it?"

"Not really, no," Ryan said. "She looks great, but jeez Louise, it's kind of scary to see her look so different."

"Maybe you should have gone more slowly with this," Dave suggested. "I mean, she became a different person all at once."

"It's called a makeover, Dave, not a make-over-the-course-of-two-weeks," Traci said.

Dave shrugged. "Well, she looks great, and she seems to be having a good time."

We all looked over at her at the seventh-grade table, and it was true. She was smiling and laughing, looking totally thrilled.

It also looked like there were a ton of boys milling around right nearby, trying to get her attention.

"Dave, I was thinking," Ryan said. "Do you want to come over to my house for a sleepover this weekend?"

Dave chuckled. "Could you give me a makeover?" he asked. We all started laughing.

"I could do your hair. I think it would look great if we put mousse in it and blow-dried it. And I have a great outfit you could try on. It's a T-shirt and a pair of jeans, and I know it will look *fabulous* on you. Also I have a great pair of tennis shoes that I think would go with it."

"It sounds great, Ryan," Dave said. "And I could brush my teeth and floss, and I'd be a whole new person."

"The girls will go crazy," Ryan said. "Amanda, you'll have to keep him handcuffed to you."

I had to admit, they were really funny, and their jokes brought me out of my bad mood for a minute. But then I looked over at Felicia, having a great time with Serena and the seventh graders, and I couldn't help feeling like I had accidentally given away my chance to be in that crowd.

I had given my chance to Felicia.

chapter
six

CHORUS FALL CONCERT AUDITIONS!

When?   Friday at 3:30 p.m.

Where? The auditorium.

Why?   Because singing lifts the spirit and heals the soul!

Who?   Anyone! You don't have to be in chorus to try out for the concert! Sing in the barbershop quartet, the girls a cappella chamber chorus, or the Madrigal choir or do a popular music solo!

The concert is November 16 at 5:00 p.m.

If you can't try out, then come to the show!

Every day that week Felicia came to school in her new look, and she seemed to be gaining more confidence every day. She also kept eating lunch with Serena and her friends and hanging out with Serena after school, too.

By Thursday, Felicia didn't seem very uncomfortable anymore. In fact, she was acting like she owned the school. On Thursday morning I was at Traci's locker with Traci and Amanda when Felicia came waltzing down the hall.

"Hey, you guys!" she said breezily.

After just three days in her new persona, she had managed to completely transform. She didn't seem the least bit nervous.

"You look great, Felicia. Did you get new clothes?" Traci asked her.

"Yeah, actually. I went shopping with Penny. She talked my dad into buying me a bunch of new stuff. You know, I'm starting to kind of like having her around."

Felicia's clothes were really nice, but I noticed that she'd copied my style pretty much to the *T*. She was wearing a pair of flared jeans, with the same boots she had on Monday, and a tight striped top with a low collar. She looked nothing like her former self.

In fact, she looked a lot like me.

"That belt looks a lot like mine but in green," I noticed out loud.

"Oh, yeah! It's exactly the same as yours. I always loved yours," she said. "I also got those jeans you have. You know, the faded ones with the zigzag pattern on the pockets?"

"Yeah, I know them," I said. I made a mental note to donate them to the Salvation Army. *Well*, I tried to tell myself, *you know what they say . . . imitation is the highest form of flattery.*

"So how've you been, Felicia? I feel like we haven't seen you in forever," Amanda said.

"I know, I'm sorry! I've been having so much fun, and it's all so brand-new and everything. I hope I haven't made you guys feel bad," Felicia said.

"No way," Traci said. "We're really happy for you. We just miss you."

"Yeah, exactly," Amanda said. "Will you please eat lunch with us today?"

"I'm so sorry," Felicia said. "I already promised I'd eat with Serena."

"Oh. Well, that's okay, then," Traci said, sounding disappointed.

"But how about if I meet you guys after school? Then we can all hang out a little," she said.

"That sounds great," Amanda said. "How about on the lawn, after the bell?"

"Okay, yeah. That's perfect," Felicia said. "Is that good for you guys?" she asked me and Traci.

"For sure," Traci said. "I'll see you there."

There was no way I was going. "Um, I already have a previous engagement. Sorry. I told Mr. Jarvis I'd help him empty trash cans in the classrooms. So I'll have to pass."

I knew I was just being rude. Obviously I would never help the janitor with the trash, but I wanted

Felicia to think that I would rather play with trash than meet her to hang out.

Felicia laughed a little, nervously, and Traci and Amanda gave me dirty looks, but I didn't care.

I was fuming.

Not only was Felicia copying my style and getting all this attention on the basis of my hard work and expertise; she also had the nerve to horn in on Serena Whitmore and her crowd, who I had been slowly and carefully working on becoming friends with since the very beginning of the year.

Felicia had totally stolen my spot. It wasn't like Serena was going to hang around with an unlimited number of sixth graders. There was probably only room for one. And now Felicia was the one and not me.

It wasn't fair. She wasn't going to get away with it.

Part of me knew that I was just jealous and that she hadn't really done anything I wouldn't do myself. But the other part of me was so mad, I could eat nails.

At lunch I had to watch Felicia sitting at Serena's table again for the fourth day in a row. It nearly made me crazy.

Traci and Amanda acted like nothing was wrong, though, and that made me crazy, too.

I had to sit at the table with Traci and Ryan and Amanda and Dave. They were all laughing and joking and having a great time. I was the fifth wheel, and I was in a really bad mood.

I took out my sushi and set it up on the table in front of me, but I wasn't hungry at all.

"So, Arielle, are you ready for the chorus concert auditions tomorrow?" Traci asked me.

Actually, this was the only topic that could cheer me up.

"Yes! I'm so excited," I told her. "I've been practicing like crazy. I have all the dance moves down perfectly."

"You're going to dance?" Traci asked.

"Yeah, of course," I said. "What do you mean? How can I do a Shauna song without dancing?"

"I don't think my mother is expecting anyone to dance," Traci said with a funny look.

Dave agreed. "I think if you start dancing like Shauna, our mother is going to freak out. I mean, all that hip wiggling and jumping around? Are you going to do all that?"

"*Yes*, I am," I insisted. "I'm going to dance exactly like Shauna, and your mom better get ready because I'm going to be amazing."

I was, too. I was working really hard to practice for the show because the concert had turned into more for me than just a way to get the attention of Eric Rich.

I was determined to get back the attention of the entire school.

I'd had enough of Felicia moving in on my position, and this concert was the perfect way to remind everyone that there was more to me than just being Felicia Fiol's former friend.

"I went shopping last night, and I got *the* most incredible outfit. I'm going to look exactly like Shauna herself," I told the rest of the table.

"Well, maybe not exactly like her, I'm guessing," Ryan said. "She's blond and like six feet tall—"

"Be quiet, Ryan," I said.

"Yeah, be quiet," Traci agreed, but she was laughing a little.

I should have known they wouldn't understand.

I had my plan, and I knew it was going to work.

I was going to get up in front of the entire school, in my most amazing outfit, looking ten times better than Felicia, and I was going to sing like Shauna. Nobody would forget who I was ever again.

The only thing standing between me and total popularity was the audition tomorrow, and that was a piece of cake. I knew nobody would dare go up against me. I had made sure everybody in chorus knew I was going to try out, and chorus wasn't exactly a class for big winners. None of them would dare cross me by trying to take the song away from me. I was psyched.

In fact, just thinking about it put me in a much better mood.

"So, you guys, will you come to the audition tomorrow and watch me try out? I would feel so much better if you were out there rooting for me," I said as the bell rang for class.

"Sure, of course we will, Ari," Amanda said.

"Yeah, I'll be there," Traci said.

"And I'm trying out, too, actually," Ryan said. "And I'll also be dressing like Shauna and doing the dance moves. So you can't get rid of me. Although you may want to."

I ran into Traci and Amanda on the way out of the building after school. I was going home to practice, and they were going to meet Felicia.

"Just come with us and hang out with her," Amanda said. "You're making too big of a deal out of this."

"No thanks," I told her. "I'll hang out with you guys until she shows up, but then I'm leaving."

"You know, you would do the exact same thing she's doing, hanging out with Serena. In fact, you *have* done it to us. You should give her a break," Amanda said.

"Okay. I will. Arm or leg?" I joked.

"Whatever," Amanda replied, sitting down on the grass.

We sat and talked for a while about our homework assignment for science. We had to come up with an experiment that proved the existence of surface tension on water, and Traci and Amanda were explaining to me what surface tension was since I didn't pay much attention in class.

After a while we noticed that the school yard was deserted. It was getting late, and Felicia still hadn't shown up.

"Maybe she got held after class," Traci said.

"Or maybe she blew you guys off," I said. "Maybe now she thinks she's too cool to meet you after school like she said she would."

"Arielle, why do you have to be so negative all the time?" Amanda asked.

But then her new red cell phone rang. Amanda smiled. I knew she loved that cell phone.

"I bet that's her!" she said.

She picked up, and Traci and I could hear only half of the conversation.

"Hey, I knew it was you!" Amanda said. Then, "Uh–huh . . . well, where are you? . . . Oh, really? Well, that's okay, I guess. . . . Yeah, I'll tell her. . . . Okay, have fun. . . . Talk to you later."

Amanda didn't say anything right away when she got off the phone, and I was feeling pretty triumphant.

"Well?" I said. It was obvious that Felicia had ditched them again.

"Um, she's at the mall with Serena. She says she's really sorry and she'll see us tomorrow."

"Really?" Traci said. "At the mall? Well, did she just

forget about us completely, or did she just decide to ditch us?" I could tell she was mad, which was rare for her.

"She promises to make it up to us later, she said. She says she forgot. And I guess we should give her the benefit of the doubt, right?" Amanda said.

"Yeah, give her the benefit of the doubt even though she's blown you off every day this week. Good plan, Amanda," I said sarcastically.

"Let's not talk about this now," Traci said. *"We're all together, right? Let's just go and have some fun. What should we do?"*

"Hey, I know. Do you guys want to come over and help me practice for the audition tomorrow?"

"All right. That sounds like fun," Traci said.

"Yeah, I'm up for that," Amanda said.

We took the bus to my house and grabbed some sodas and snacks from the fridge.

Anya, our Russian housekeeper, yelled at us on our way up the stairs for coming in the house with shoes on, but I just gave her a smile and pretended not to understand what she was saying.

I shut and locked the door to my room to avoid any more interruptions and got ready to show them my moves.

"Okay, you guys, why don't I just pretend you're Ms. McClintic and I'll do a dress rehearsal for the audition?"

"That won't be too hard. Traci looks just like her!" Amanda said, and Traci laughed.

I put on one of the possible outfits I was thinking about wearing to the audition. I wanted to look good, but not too good, for the tryout. I was saving my best, most spectacular clothes for the concert.

I put on a pair of tight stretchy jeans that flared a little at the bottom and some sandals with chunky heels. I had a little top that showed my belly button and came down off one shoulder but was tight enough that it wouldn't fly around while I danced.

"You look great!" Traci said. "Just like Shauna."

"Thanks," I told her. "Plus, you have to picture it. I'm going to do my hair like this," I said, holding it up.

"That'll look great," Amanda said. "Let's hear you sing the song."

I went over to my stereo and put on my Shauna CD. I found the right song and turned the volume way up.

When the first notes of the song started, I jumped up into my first dance move and then just went with it. I had a whole routine choreographed that I had copied from Shauna's video, and I danced and sang along with the music as loud as I could.

"That was great!" Amanda said when I was finished. She and Traci clapped and clapped. I was sweating, and I caught a look at myself in the mirror as I was beginning to cool down.

I did look great, I thought.

"Isn't it going to be hard to sing while you're dancing so hard?" Traci asked.

"No, I don't think so. Shauna does it," I said.

"But she has a sound system and a microphone attached to her head," Amanda pointed out.

"Yeah, but that's for a much bigger auditorium and with a whole band behind her. I'll just have the piano," I explained.

"Okay, let's hear you do it," Amanda said.

I went back over to the stereo to turn the song back on, but Traci said, "No, no. You have to let us hear you *sing* it, without the stereo. This is a dress rehearsal, remember?"

"Oh, yeah, okay," I said.

I got into position to start the dance . . . and one and two and three . . . and I started dancing and singing at the same time. I sang as I danced, and I could hear that it was really breathy, and I was panting. I got through it, but I was really out of breath.

When I finished, I looked over at Traci and Amanda. They looked horrified.

"Come on, you guys, it wasn't that bad, was it?" I asked.

"Um, I think you should try singing it without dancing so we can hear what you really sound like. It's hard to tell when you're moving all around like that," Traci said.

"Okay. I'll just sing it," I said.

The song was "You Owe Me, Baby," off Shauna's fourth album. I knew it by heart, but as I started singing, I realized I had never sung it without the CD before. The sound of my own voice wasn't as great as I had imagined it would be.

After I was done, Traci and Amanda clapped again. But this time it seemed more like they were doing it to be polite.

"Let me give you some quick pointers on breathing from your diaphragm," Traci offered. "This might be the only time that having my mom be a music teacher is useful to me."

But I didn't want any pointers, really. I realized what the problem was. In the audition I would be accompanied by the piano. I had trouble singing it like this because there was no music to guide me.

"No, you know what it is, you guys? I don't sound good because I have no music with me. Once I have the piano playing along with me, I'll have no trouble at all," I said, smiling.

"Are you sure you don't want to just take a couple of quick pointers?" Traci asked.

"Yeah, maybe just give it a try, Arielle," Amanda said.

"No, no, I'm okay. Just wait until you see the whole thing put together, with piano music, and up on the stage, not here in my room. I'm gonna look great," I said.

"But, Arielle, it's kind of more about how you sound than how you look," Traci said.

"Well, *I'm* more interested in how I look. And look at it this way: No one is trying out but me, so I'll get the part and then I can work on how I sound up until the concert," I rationalized. "I'm not worried at all."

chapter
SEVEN

Note on Felicia's locker

Hey, Felish—
 I'll meet you at the water fountain in front of the auditorium at 3:45 for the *BIG SURPRISE!* You are going to do great!
         Luv, Serena

I was so excited about the audition all day at school, I could hardly pay attention in class. I got in trouble with pretty much *every* teacher for spacing out.

Science was the worst. I thought I had gotten the concept of surface tension down, but it turned out I still had it wrong.

"Who can give me an example of surface tension in action?" the teacher asked.

I raised my hand. I usually don't volunteer, but I had just been learning about it from Amanda and Traci, and besides, I was in a really good mood.

"Yes, Arielle, nice to see you involved in class."

"An example of surface tension is when you put a paper

70

clip in water and it sinks to the bottom," I said proudly.

"Well, no, Arielle, not really. Actually, that's the opposite of surface tension. Thanks for trying, though."

Oh, well, I thought. *I knew there was something about a paper clip in there somewhere.*

Instead of going to lunch that afternoon, I went to the dance room to practice my moves.

The dance room was a great space with mirrors on all four walls, so I could see myself clearly and make sure I wasn't making any mistakes. I was alone in there, and I watched myself in the mirror as I did the routine over and over again. I knew I looked great, and after a while I started to sing the actual song along with the dance moves.

I didn't think I sounded half bad.

After the workout I was even more excited, and I had to rush to get to class on time.

I ran into Felicia in the hallway. She was coming out of the bathroom, where she must have been freshening her makeup.

"Hi," I said to her, pretty coldly.

"Hey, Arielle," she said, looking excited. If she noticed that I was acting cold, it didn't show. "I'm glad I ran into you. I really wanted to talk to you about something."

"Yeah, what?" I asked.

"Well, I—I'm actually—the thing is . . ." she stammered.

Then the second bell rang, meaning we were late for class.

"Guess we don't have time, Felicia. I'll see you later," I said, and walked away.

"Wait!" she called.

I turned around and looked at her.

"Actually . . ." she said, looking at me, "never mind." And then she turned around herself and walked away.

I decided right there and then that I was not going to speak to her anymore. Then I spun on my heel and walked to my class.

After class I had to move fast to get to the auditions on time.

I ran to my locker and got my bag of gear and then rushed to the girls' locker room to get ready.

I took a really quick shower and then dried my hair a little and put it up in the same kind of French twist that Shauna wears. I had taught myself how to do this hairdo from an article in a magazine that I read, and it had taken me only two tries to get it perfect. I took out the small makeup mirror from my bag and admired my handiwork from the back. It was just right.

Then I did my makeup. I took off the makeup I was wearing and reapplied some brighter makeup that I thought would look good under the lights of the auditorium.

Finally, I got changed. I was planning to wear a

cropped sleeveless turtleneck to show off my arms and a pair of stretchy yoga pants that were perfect for dancing.

When I had everything together, I went and checked myself in the long mirror.

Perfect!

I rushed upstairs to meet Traci and Amanda by the auditorium.

"You look so great!" Amanda said as I walked up. "I'm waiting here for Ryan and Traci."

"I feel great," I said. "I just know this is going to be totally awesome."

"Hey, Amanda, hey, Shauna," Ryan said as he walked up.

I giggled.

"Whoa! Arielle, I totally thought Shauna Ferris was here hanging out with Amanda. From behind you're a dead ringer."

"Shut up, Ryan!" I said, but I laughed, anyway. This was going to be the greatest day ever.

Today I was going to win back my position as the most popular girl in the sixth grade.

Of course I would never talk like that in front of Traci and Amanda. They wouldn't understand. Actually, the only person who understood stuff the same way I did was Felicia.

Suddenly, I really missed her. After all, she was one of my best friends, even if she was acting like a jerk.

"Here comes Traci," Amanda said. "Come on, let's go in so we can get a good seat."

I saw Ryan and Traci smile at each other as she walked up.

"Cool outfit," Traci said to me.

"Thanks," I said happily.

We sat down in the front of the darkened auditorium, all in the same row. I was sitting between Amanda and Traci, and I thought for a second how lucky I was to have such good friends to hang out with.

"Hello, everybody! Thanks so much for coming," Ms. McClintic said. "We're going to start with auditions for the barbershop quartet. Can I have the altos and tenors come up, please?"

We sat through everyone's tryout, clapping and cheering for the people we knew. It was pretty interesting, actually. Traci kept shushing me whenever I tried to make fun of someone. Some people were really terrible, though.

Ryan went up and sang the song he was trying out for. He had a beautiful voice, and Ms. McClintic smiled as he sang.

It wasn't too hard to tell that he would definitely get the song.

"You were great! Really great," I said when he came back down to his seat. Traci was beaming at him. I never really had feelings for him one way or the other, but I could see just then why she liked him.

The Shauna song was the very last of the audition, so we had to wait through the entire thing to get to me.

By the time my turn came up, I practically jumped out of my seat.

"Thank you, Arielle," Ms. McClintic said as I came up onstage. For the first time I felt a tiny bit nervous.

"For some reason I can't figure out, nobody else signed up for this song, Arielle, so it looks like this audition is just for fun—you've definitely got the part."

"Really? No one else? That's funny," I said, although I knew full well that nobody had the guts to go up against me.

"Let's give it a go, anyway, just to see how you sound, okay?"

"Yes, great! I'm ready!"

I could see Traci and Amanda smiling at me from the audience.

I got into position for the spin that started the dance routine as Ms. McClintic went to the piano.

She gave me a funny look when she saw the position I was in, kind of crouched over and turned to the side, but I figured she'd understand as soon as she started playing.

She began, and I started my routine. But she was playing *way* too slow!

I stopped. "Ms. McClintic, do you think you could play a little faster? That's not really how the song goes."

"Okay . . . sure, Arielle. Um, let's try it again."

She started again at the right tempo, and I took off

dancing and moving, singing as loudly as I could. I could hear that my voice was a little off, and I was kind of out of breath, but I kept going because I was really in a groove with the dancing.

Then Ms. McClintic stopped.

"Arielle, honey," she said. "I love your dancing, but I'm having trouble hearing you sing."

I stopped, frustrated. I should have known Ms. McClintic, who knew nothing about Shauna, wouldn't be able to appreciate the dancing.

I mean, Shauna was not *about* the singing, really. She was about the presentation, the show, the look. And that was what I was going to bring to this concert, which would otherwise be completely boring and lame. Ms. McClintic had never seen a Shauna video in her life, and so she had no idea of even the concept I was going for.

But still, I didn't want to be rude.

"Okay, no problem, Ms. McClintic. Do you want me to slow down some of my dance moves?"

"Well, let's try it just standing still, okay? And let's start over because you were a little flat last time."

Hmph. So I sang the song standing still. I figured I'd have the next couple of weeks to get her used to the idea of my dancing. Heck, maybe we could even get a sound system set up so that I could have a microphone like Shauna.

I knew I didn't sound great, but I wasn't terrible, either. I knew all the words, and I basically knew the tune. The piano covered up most of the mistakes I made, I thought.

Ms. McClintic played the final chords of the song, and I did a spin and a kick, just for good measure.

My friends cheered like crazy, even though I knew I didn't sound great. But it didn't matter whether I was great right now. No matter what, I would be great at the concert, and that's all that mattered.

"Thanks, Arielle, and congratulations. We can do some work with your voice before the concert," Ms. McClintic said.

I hopped off the stage as everybody started getting up. The audition was over.

"Great job, Arielle," Traci said, putting her arm around me.

But then there was a commotion at the door of the auditorium.

I saw Serena Whitmore and a bunch of the seventh-grade girls murmuring and making encouraging sounds.

"Go on!" I heard someone say. "You can do it."

Suddenly, *Felicia* came through the door and walked halfway down the aisle, pushed by a crowd of seventh graders!

What the heck?!

Ms. McClintic turned around from packing up her music at the piano.

"Ms. McClintic?" Felicia called. "Is it too late to try out for the Shauna Ferris solo?"

Traci and Amanda gasped next to me.

"No, not at all, hon. Come on up," Ms. McClintic said.

Felicia went up to the stage as Ms. McClintic took her seat at the piano again.

Traci and Amanda and I sat with our mouths open, stunned, as this whole thing unfolded.

How could she do this to me?

The seventh graders settled into seats near the front, and Ms. McClintic started playing. She played the song slowly, and Felicia's voice filled the auditorium with the most beautiful rendition of Shauna I had ever heard. I had no idea that Felicia had such a great voice.

I knew she knew all the words to every Shauna song because I had taught them to her, but who knew she could sing on her own?

Felicia, with her new hair and new makeup and new clothes, had somehow turned into this person I didn't know, who was really confident and had an amazing singing voice.

When she finished, the room erupted in applause. Everyone cheered except me and Amanda and Traci. Ryan started to applaud, but Traci elbowed him and he stopped.

"Thank you so much for coming," Ms. McClintic said. "That was beautiful, Felicia. You'll have to come and try out for chorus."

Felicia went back over to her new friends, and they

all hugged her and told her how great she was.

"Sorry," Amanda said to me. "I can't believe it."

"I know," Traci said as we watched the group, with Felicia at the center, go out the auditorium door. "I can't believe she would do that," Traci went on. "That was so uncool. She knew you really wanted to do the song."

"To try out without even telling you is so rude," Amanda said.

I felt like crying, but I knew what I had to do. I wouldn't cry. I would get a plan. A plan to win back my place—the place that Felicia had stolen.

But first I had to wait and see whether or not I would get the part. It was true Felicia had a better singing voice, but I definitely had much better presentation. Who knew if Ms. McClintic would appreciate that, though?

chapter
EIGHT

Credit card bill for Arielle's trip to the mall

Shoemania: black boots, $52.50
Fashion Connection: miniskirt and sweater, $126.00
The Leather Shoppe: belt, $79.00
Spin Doctor: new Shauna single, DVD of Shauna videos, $17.89

"So who can tell us the value of X?" asked Mr. Reid. "Arielle? You look like you're dying to tell us what X is."

He was trying to be snide. I had been looking out the window, obviously not paying attention at all. But I didn't have the energy to come up with a snide retort, like I usually do.

"Sorry, I wasn't paying attention, Mr. Reid."

"You don't say?" he said in an arch tone.

I went back to looking out the window.

The audition results were going to be posted at the end of the day in the music room, and I could think of nothing else.

The day dragged on and on, and when lunch

finally came, I felt like I had already been through three days of school.

I sat down with Amanda and Traci at our table, but I was not in the mood to make conversation.

"So I tried to ask my mom last night who was going to get the Shauna song," Traci said to me.

Finally, a topic that interested me!

"Really? What did she say?" I demanded.

"She wouldn't tell me. You know how she is." Traci imitated her mother. "'It wouldn't be fair of me to put you in the position of knowing more than you should because you are the daughter of a faculty member . . .' and all that."

"Well, but what do you think she's going to do? Did you tell her what a traitor Felicia was by trying out?" I asked her, starting to get mad again. "Did you tell her that even though Felicia has a nice voice, she's a bad friend, and we're going to boo her so loud if she gets the part that no one will be able to hear what she's singing?"

"Arielle, don't get so freaked out," Amanda said to me. "Let's just wait and see what happens, okay? Maybe you'll get it."

But then I saw her and Traci exchange a look that told me they didn't think I was going to.

"Listen," Amanda said. "I talked to Felicia on the phone last night, and she said she felt bad about going behind your back, but she really wanted to try out, and she said she tried to tell you in the hall Friday at school, but she was too scared."

"She *should* have been afraid. That song was mine!" I said. "Wait a minute. You talked to her on the phone?"

"Yeah," Amanda said. "She called me."

"And you took her call? She's a traitor," I said.

"I know you're upset, Arielle. But maybe you should talk to her."

"I'll see you girls later," I said, and got up. I couldn't sit there anymore. I was going crazy.

I took my Walkman and went and sat on the front steps in the sun and listened to Shauna. If I was going to be miserable, at least I could get a tan. My mother always yells at me to wear sunscreen. She says if I don't, I'll regret it later, when I start getting wrinkles, but I figure by the time I'm that age, they'll have invented some pill that stops your skin from wrinkling.

When the bell rang, I kept my Walkman on and went to my next class. My plan was to sit in the back and try to keep it on through the whole class.

Of course it didn't work, and I was forced to listen to forty-five minutes of droning on about the Revolutionary War in my social studies class.

Somehow I got through the rest of the day, and when the final bell rang, it was time for me to go and check the chorus concert list.

My mind was racing as I walked down the hall to the music room off the auditorium. The hallways had never seemed so long.

On the one hand, I was sure I got the song. My voice wasn't great, but it wasn't terrible, either. And my presentation—the show I put on—was excellent. A part of me was sure that Ms. McClintic could appreciate that on some level.

On the other hand, I could just see Ms. McClintic, knowing nothing whatsoever about the Shauna phenomenon, being totally impressed with Felicia the traitor's pretty little singing voice and giving the song to her.

It was enough to make my hair curl.

A crowd gathered around the list. I crossed the room and pushed people aside to get up close to see it.

My eyes scanned down the list to the bottom. My heart sank.

Next to Shauna Ferris's "You Owe Me, Baby" was the name Felicia Fiol.

I was suddenly so mad, I felt like screaming or hitting someone. I spun around and stormed away, pushing people aside as I walked. "Hey!" someone said as I slammed into them. I didn't even apologize.

I walked out of the building without even stopping to get my books. Who cared about homework when my life was over? I went straight home.

I walked in the door, and Anya yelled at me again

about my shoes, but I didn't even pretend not to understand her. I just went straight up to my room, turned on Shauna full volume, flopped down on my bed, and cried.

I stayed that way for a long time.

My phone rang, but I ignored it. The machine picked up, and it was Amanda and Traci, calling from Amanda's cell.

"Hey, Ari, it's us. We were looking everywhere for you. I guess you saw the list. We're so sorry. I hope you're okay, and we want to take you out for ice cream or something. Call us as soon as you get this."

I cried a little more because their message was so nice. How could Felicia have done this to me? Life was so unfair!

After a couple of hours I started to pull myself together. Listening to Shauna always made me feel better.

I got up off the bed and started to do some dance moves in the mirror.

Then I got more into it, and I danced and danced until I was sweaty and much, much happier.

I remembered my promise to myself to turn my anger and rage into a plan. Now a plan started to formulate itself in my mind.

The music was still turned up as loud as it would go, and I didn't hear the banging on my door until my mom started yelling.

"For Pete's sake, Arielle! Turn it down! What are you doing in there?"

I turned it down and opened the door.

"Sorry, Mom," I said. I was glad to see her because I needed some things from her to make my plan work.

"Listen, hon," she said, talking quickly. "I thought we'd all have dinner together, sound good?" She was talking in what I call her "office voice" —it was quick and short, wasting no words. She sounded like she was in a big hurry.

"We who? Is Dad coming home?" I asked. I hoped so. I would need him on my side for this one, but he rarely came home for dinner.

"Yes. He'll be home in thirty minutes. Anya cooked something for dinner. We'll sit down at seven, okay?" Her cell phone rang. She was holding it in her hand like she was expecting a call. "Oh, shoot. Just a second. Hello? Great, do you have those numbers yet? . . ." She wandered off down the hall, I guess discussing a contract of some sort.

Both of my parents are corporate lawyers, and they work all the time, even when they're home.

I met them in the dining room at seven. My dad was already sitting down, but he had his laptop open next to him on the table.

"Hi, honey! How are you?" he asked. He closed his computer and turned to me. "Isn't this nice? To have dinner together?"

"It sure is, Dad. I'm good, how are you?" I asked.

"Oh, just fine, honey."

My mom walked in, still on the phone. "Yes, tell them yes, but only if there's a cut for us on the back end. It's boilerplate, so I'm not too worried. Okay, I'm hanging up. Bye."

She clicked her phone shut and set it on the table next to her.

"Well. This looks good. Yum," she said in her work voice.

"It does indeed," my dad said. "Thank you, Anya," he said as she brought one more dish in and set it down on the table.

He began serving himself.

"So tell us about school, Ari," my mom asked, taking some meat from the platter my dad handed her. She was still in her suit, and she glanced at her phone as she was asking me. She must be waiting for a call.

"Well, I did pretty well on that science test I was telling you about. You know, the one about the properties of water?"

Actually I had gotten a D, but they didn't need to know that. It would just worry them.

"Terrific. Good job," my mom said, and then her phone rang again. "Sorry, guys," she said to us. "Hello . . . yes . . . no, that's not going to work. I need you to give it more of a spin toward the . . . exactly . . ." she went on.

"So tell me what else is happening, hon. How's soccer?" my dad said, talking over my mom on her cell.

"Oh, it's great, Dad. Did I tell you I scored a goal

in the game against Washington last week? And we won by one point!"

"That's my girl. Way to go, Ari," he said through a mouthful of chicken.

Finally, my mom hung up the phone, and I saw my chance.

"You guys, I wanted to talk to you about something. There are two things I really want, and I need to ask you about them."

"Sure, honey, what is it?" my mom asked. Usually, they were really generous, and I had no trouble at all when I wanted something.

"Well, the first thing I want is just to go clothes shopping again. I need to find something really, really killer to wear. And the other thing is that I want to take voice lessons."

"Hmmm," my dad said. "You want voice lessons, huh? Does this have anything to do with the song you were trying out for in the school concert?"

"Yes, exactly, Daddy. I didn't get the song, and I want to ask if I can try out again after I have some voice lessons. I'm pretty sure Ms. McClintic will give me another chance."

"Hon, I really don't think we can justify your taking voice lessons for just one song," my mother said. She was still in courtroom mode. I should have waited until she had a chance to wind down a little.

"It's not just one song, Mom. It's every time I sing

for the rest of my life. Isn't there some value to music for music's sake?"

That was a good one, I thought. I was sure they'd go for it.

"Come on, Arielle." My mother snorted. She could see right through me.

"Listen, Ari. I agree with your mother. I just don't see you being serious about studying voice. I think we have to say no."

"Yes." My mother continued the shutout. "And as for going shopping for new clothes, Arielle, you went to the mall and spent a fortune just a couple of days ago."

"Yes, but that was before I knew exactly what I was looking for," I explained.

"Well, honey, plan ahead next time," my dad said. "Now, let's eat."

I couldn't believe it! Did I have a sign on my forehead that said LOSER? I was getting nothing but dumped on today by everybody. First the Shauna song, and now my parents were saying no to me about the simplest thing.

Oh, well, I thought. I would just have to try them again in a few days when they were in a better mood. Maybe I'd go with the one-at-a-time tactic. I'd just have to figure out who would be first.

If there was anything I was sure of in life, it was that if you keep trying, you can always get what you want.

chapter
NINE

Sign-up sheet hanging in children's ward of the Wonder Lake Memorial Hospital

HEALING PAWS PROGRAM

Please sign here if you would like your child to participate in the weekly Healing Paws animal program. A group of volunteers from the local animal shelter will bring in the animal of your child's choice for him or her to play with. Please indicate child's name and favorite type of animal.

1. Rodney Chivres—cats
2. Melanie Oppenweil—cats or kittens
3. Sarah Kinn—ferret (or puppy if you don't have one)
4. George Walters—horse or cat or dog
5. Cameron Gale—don't care—any kind
6. Justin Havlick—rats or mice

I was late getting to lunch on Wednesday because Mr. Reid made me stay after class to redo my homework, which was all wrong, so I was in a horrible mood by the time I got to lunch.

Actually, I had been in a horrible mood all week. What, exactly, did I have to be in a good mood about? My formerly best friend had betrayed me, stolen my friends and my song; my parents were acting like I was some spoiled brat and refusing to give me anything I wanted. It couldn't get any worse, I thought.

That's what I thought, anyway, until I walked into the lunchroom.

Felicia had finally decided to grace us with her presence at our usual table. She was sitting by the window with Traci, Amanda, Ryan, and Dave.

"Hey, Arielle!" Traci called to me, as if nothing was wrong.

I gave her a cold stare. How dare they allow the traitor to sit with them?

Looking around the lunchroom quickly for a new place to sit, I got a gift from God. There was a spot open at the seventh-grader table, right next to Serena.

I decided to sit there. Even though I hadn't talked to them since they started hanging out with Felicia, they were *my* friends in the first place.

I made tracks over to the spot to grab it before somebody else took it.

"Hey, Arielle," Serena said as I walked up. "How are you? Have a seat."

"I'm good. Great, actually. How about you?" I took out my sushi and laid it out on the table.

"I'm good," she said.

"I really like your shirt," I told her. It was a turtleneck with gold piping on the sleeves. "Where'd you get it?"

"Oh, this is Felicia's," Serena said. "I slept over at her house on Saturday, and she lent it to me."

I couldn't believe it. I couldn't believe Serena slept at Felicia's, and I couldn't believe Felicia had such a cool shirt.

"Oh, cool," I said with a tight smile.

"You know, I'm sorry you didn't get the Shauna song in the concert. I hope you weren't too bummed about it," she said.

"No. I mean, sure, I was bummed, but I was glad Felicia got it," I lied. "I never knew she had such a nice voice."

"I know, doesn't she?" Serena said.

"She really does sound great," another girl sitting next to us said. "She kind of sounds better than Shauna herself."

Uh-uh, I thought. Better than Shauna. I didn't think so. Not in this lifetime.

"Dude, you were totally looking at her! Ha-ha-ha!" A boy was teasing loudly. I looked down the table and saw Patrick, the gangly kid who had been checking me out last week, blushing and punching his friend who was teasing him.

Serena leaned in toward me. "Patrick likes Felicia," she told me in a whisper. "They're giving him a hard time about it."

"Do you think she likes him?" I asked, my brain clicking.

"Yeah, I think she does," Serena said. "Don't tell her I told you," she added, laughing.

What did I care if some scrawny guy liked her instead of me? She was welcome to my rejects anytime.

"Did you hear that he asked Felicia to go to the movies this weekend?" the girl to Serena's right asked her.

"Yeah. And she said yes, I think, if her father will let her," Serena said.

"Her father's really strict?" the girl asked.

"Yeah, a little," Serena answered. "But he's really cool. They live on kind of a farm that's an animal shelter, and at her house there are all these animals around. It's awesome."

I couldn't believe I was sitting there listening to them talk about my former good friend. And I couldn't believe I was sitting with Serena and all she could talk about was my archenemy, Felicia.

"We had such a good time this weekend," Serena said. "We went to the mall and there was a huge sale at Mosley's and I got four new things. Felicia helped me pick them out. She has such a great sense of style, you know. . . ." And on and on Serena went about Felicia. *Great sense of style?* I was the one who gave her this supposed great sense of style.

I finished eating and prayed for lunch to end soon.

Then I saw Felicia wave good-bye to Traci and

Amanda at our regular table and leave the lunch-room. I was saved.

"Well, it was great talking to you guys. I have to go and study for a test, so I'll see you later," I said to Serena, and got up to go.

"Okay. Bye, Arielle, good to see you!"

I went over to talk to Amanda and Traci. I was kind of mad at them for eating lunch with Felicia, but when I got there, I found that they were kind of mad at her, too.

"We asked her to do something with us this week-end, and she said she had to check with her other friends first to make sure she had time," Traci told me. "Can you believe that?"

"Yes," I said simply. "She's a traitor and a bad friend. This is news to you guys?"

"All right. Let's not get carried away," Amanda said. "We're not going to talk about her like that."

"Why not? She deserves it."

"No, she doesn't. Listen, you guys, no matter what, we know that we'll all get a chance to hang out together at Healing Paws on Saturday."

"Right," said Traci.

"Right. So let's plan to talk to her about all this before it starts. I mean, we'll all sit down, face-to-face. I'm sure we can solve this problem if we just talk it through," Amanda said.

"Whatever." I shrugged. "Hey, did you guys know that Felicia likes Patrick and he likes her, too?"

"Yeah, she told us," Amanda said. "She thought she might go to the movies with him this weekend."

"That's what Serena said. In fact, Serena and her friends talked about Felicia the entire time we were eating," I said.

"Really? What else did they say?" asked Traci.

"They said how great it was that Felicia had such a great voice and how sad it was that I didn't," I said bitterly.

"Oh, no, they did not," Traci said. "But I'm sorry, anyway, if they brought it up."

"Thanks," I said. "Did you know that Serena spent the night at Felicia's last weekend?"

"No way! She did?" Amanda asked.

"Yeah," I said, "and she just spent the entire lunch telling the entire table how great it was there, with the animals and all, and how cool Mr. Fiol is."

"Oh, man, that's so weird. It's like Felicia has a whole new life that we don't know about," Traci said.

"Exactly. So do you see why I'm in such a bad mood about all this?" I asked them.

"Yeah, I get it. But listen. We can work this out—I'm sure of it. We'll talk to her out at her place before Healing Paws," Amanda said.

"And this is going to be the best Healing Paws yet!" Traci said. "I miss the kids so much. I can't wait to see them."

"I know. Me too," Amanda said. "And I'm sure Felicia feels the same way."

Traci nodded and grinned. "I have a feeling that on Saturday we're going to finally see the good old Felicia again."

"That'd be nice," I mumbled.

"I hope so, too," said Amanda.

We walked out of the cafeteria together to go to our next classes.

"Cheer up, Arielle," Traci said to me. "I'll see you at soccer and you can take out some of your aggression on the ball."

That made me feel a little better. "Yeah, maybe I can take it out on you if we have another scrimmage," I said with a smile.

Traci and I were on the varsity soccer team, and we split the position of center forward. Lately we'd been scrimmaging, which meant that we played opposite each other. It was really fun because we were evenly matched, but we tended to get pretty fierce with each other.

Traci was right. I knew I'd feel better on the soccer field.

Coach Talbot blew her whistle on me for the third time in ten minutes.

"Arielle! Do you think you're kickboxing or something? Another stunt like that and you'll sit out the rest of the practice!"

I was being really aggressive, I knew. Sometimes on the soccer field I have trouble stopping myself from playing too rough when I'm going for the ball.

"Arielle, if you hit me again, I swear I'm going to punch you in the nose."

Traci was furious because we had just both gone for the ball at the same time, and I dove at her and knocked her down. I had knocked the wind out of her, and she had to lie there and catch her breath for five minutes. She was finally up and back in the game.

But just five minutes before, I had miscalculated a kick and ended up kicking her in the thigh really hard. I could already see the bruise coming up on her leg.

"I'm sorry, Traci."

We played on, and I fought her as hard as I could to keep control of the ball. The air was cold, and I was running so much that my lungs were burning, but it felt great to be letting off some steam.

The ball came to me, and I received it and faked out Traci to get it past her. I blew past the other side's lame defense, and even though my wing was wide open, I totally hogged the ball and went for the goal. I took my shot, and the ball hit the goalpost and bounced directly into the goalie's grasp.

That's what I got for being greedy. That and another reprimand from Coach Talbot.

"Didn't you see that Eleanor was wide open, Arielle? Try some teamwork next time."

She blew her whistle, and Traci and I faced off at center again.

"Are you all right?" Traci asked me.

"Yeah, I'm fine," I said. "Just playing a little soccer."

"Well, chill out, will you? You're going to end up benched for the next game if you keep playing like a jerk," she said.

Traci was pretty polite in real life, but she was more direct and aggressive when we were on the soccer field. But for all that, she was a real team player. She always passed at every opportunity and never showed off, even though she was probably the best player on the team.

I wished I could be more like her out there, actually.

"I know, I know," I told her. I had a reputation for being a loose cannon on the team, and I told myself to be more careful and to pass more.

It was just that every time I thought of Felicia and that stupid concert, I wanted to grab the ball and jump up and down on it until it popped.

chapter
TEN

E-mail from Traci to Amanda Wednesday night

Hey—

Just trying to get this science homework done. What did you say for question number 12? Have you heard anything from Felicia? She hasn't called or written me in three days.

Amanda's reply

I think number 12 is the prefrontal cortex, but I'm not totally sure. I haven't heard from Felicia, either. I'm glad she's having fun, though. I mean, I'm really trying to be glad for her.

I got my stuff from my locker the next morning and looked over at Traci and Amanda. They were checking their watches and conferring.

Even though Felicia wasn't available the rest of the day, up till now she'd at least hung out with us every morning at the lockers. Her locker was right nearby, and it was almost impossible to miss her.

Every morning when she showed up, I would just turn around and go the other way. But this morning, no Felicia at all.

"What's up, you guys?" I said, going over to Traci and Amanda.

"I don't know what happened to Felicia," Traci said. "I guess we should just get going so we're not late."

The day before, Traci's mom had given us a serious talking-to about being late. We were late for her homeroom so often that she said it looked like she was giving special privileges to Traci and her friends because she was Traci's mother. If we were late again, she told us, she would give us a major detention.

"Okay, let's go, then," I said.

"Wait, let me just put a note on Felicia's locker so she doesn't think we ditched her," Amanda said. She took out a sheet of paper and started scribbling on it.

"You know, more likely she ditched you two," I said.

"Arielle, don't be a jerk. We see her every morning," Amanda said, putting the note on Felicia's locker.

"Ready?" Traci asked.

We headed down the hall.

We got about fifty feet down the hall before we ran into Felicia. Or spotted her and her friends walking by us, that is.

"Hey! There you are, Felicia. What happened to you?" Amanda said to her.

But to everyone's astonishment, Felicia kept walking. She didn't stop, and she didn't even say hello.

She just smiled and waved.

Then she walked right by, still talking and chatting with her crowd of seventh-grade friends, in her new cool clothes, with her new cool hair that I taught her how to straighten.

Traci and Amanda were so shocked, they stopped walking and stared after her.

"Did you see that, too, or am I hallucinating?" Amanda said.

"No. I saw it. She just ignored us. She just smiled and waved and kept on walking," Traci said in disbelief.

I felt the thrill of victory. There was no way Traci and Amanda could keep up their good feelings about Felicia after a stunt like that.

"Wow. That was the rudest thing I've ever seen," Amanda said. "All right, I can't help it. *Now* I'm mad."

Finally! Traci and Amanda were on *my* side. Now I could get to work figuring out what my revenge plan was going to be.

We started walking again toward homeroom. Traci and Amanda didn't say one more word all the way there.

We just barely got into the room as the bell rang.

"So nice of you to join us, girls, and in such a timely manner," Ms. McClintic joked.

But none of us were much in the mood for joking.

We sat down, and the announcements started droning over the loudspeaker.

Amanda wrote huge on her notebook so Traci and I could see.

HOW COULD SHE IGNORE US LIKE THAT?

Traci wrote back in her big loopy handwriting, *I know. We've been so patient with her new friends, and now this.*

WHO DOES SHE THINK SHE IS? I MEAN, THE MAKEOVER WAS ARIELLE'S IDEA IN THE FIRST PLACE!

Finally! Some recognition. I was so happy to have my friends on my side after all this time, I didn't even butt into their complaint session.

Amanda was hunkered down over her notebook, scribbling furiously. She pushed her notebook over to the side of her desk so we could see what she'd written.

WHEN WE SEE HER AT HEALING PAWS, I'M GOING TO TELL HER EXACTLY HOW I FEEL.

Lunch was more of the same. Felicia sat with Serena and company, and we sat at our usual table without her. Felicia didn't even bother to make her

101

usual stop by our table to say hello. It looked like she was done with us.

"What I don't understand is, how the heck can she act like this? We're her best friends. Doesn't she miss us?" Amanda asked no one in particular.

Obviously, these were questions without answers.

"I know," Traci said. "It makes me really sad."

"Look at her sitting there with that guy Patrick," Amanda said, pointing at Felicia, who was between Serena and Patrick and laughing with him. "I mean, doesn't she remember that just two weeks ago he was passing by here over and over trying to get *you* to notice him, Arielle? How can she like a guy like that?"

Get you *to notice him.*

Trying to catch your *eye.* Right then my mind began to click. What I needed was a way to get to Felicia, to take away some of her self-confidence. Then I could step back into my rightful place as most popular girl in the sixth grade.

I gave Felicia the self-confidence in the first place, I told myself. *There's no reason for me not to take it away if she isn't using it properly.*

I gave her the looks that attracted Patrick, and I taught her how to use them to keep his attention. If she was going to compete with me, then I was going to compete with her. It was only fair.

But I wouldn't tell Traci and Amanda just yet. I had to let the plan develop a little more.

"So are you going to come to Healing Paws on Saturday, anyway?" Amanda asked me.

"Yeah, definitely. I'm dying to see the kids. I don't have to talk to Felicia," I said. "Are you two coming?"

We would have to go to Felicia's house for Healing Paws, to get the animals ready to bring to the hospital.

"I wouldn't miss it for anything. I'm not going to let Felicia's jerkiness ruin Healing Paws for the kids," Amanda said.

"*Jerkiness.* Is that even a word?" Traci said, laughing.

"I think so." Amanda laughed, too. "If it isn't, it should be."

"Hey, girls," Ryan said, walking up. "How's it hanging?"

"Pretty good," Traci said with a smile.

It didn't take much to cheer her up, I thought.

"Hey, what's up with Felicia?" he asked. "I passed her in the hall earlier. I said hello, and I swear she pretended she didn't see me."

"What's up is that she's an obnoxious jerk," Amanda said.

That was pretty extreme for Amanda. She almost never insulted anyone.

"Whoa, she's really in the doghouse for you to talk like that, Amanda, huh?" Ryan sat down next to Traci.

"She's not in the doghouse; she's in the pig's slop bucket. She's in the rat's hole. She's in the—"

"Okay, then. Jeez, take it easy," he said.

"We're really mad at her," Traci told him. "She's completely ignoring us like we don't even exist."

"That's bad," he agreed. "What are you going to do?"

"What can we do? We decided we'd try to talk to her on Saturday. We know we'll see her before Healing Paws," Traci explained.

"I have another plan." I spoke up. "It involves revenge. A little less conversation, a little more action, if you know what I mean."

"I'll see her in math this afternoon," Traci muttered, seeming not to hear me at all. "We always sit together. I wonder how it'll go?"

"I'll tell you how it'll go," I jumped in. "You can't sit with her. Don't look at her, and take a seat somewhere else in the room. She can't act like she did this morning and then have you talking to her the first chance you get in math class," I ranted. "She can't get away with this."

"Yeah, I guess you're right," Traci said, looking around. "But could you keep your voice down, Arielle? People are looking at us."

"Fine!" I practically shouted. "Let them look! Hello, people!" I waved like a maniac.

I was mad and behaving badly, I knew, but at least I was making Traci and Amanda laugh even though they were embarrassed.

The first bell rang, which meant it was time to start heading to class. We all got up to leave.

"Remember," I said to Traci, "don't talk to her."

"Yeah, okay, I'll try not to," she replied wearily.

We all headed off in different directions. "See you in English!" I called to Traci.

I spent my time in class formulating a plan for revenge. I did my best to look interested in what was going on so I wouldn't get called on and I could concentrate.

By the time last-period English rolled around, I had pretty much figured out what I was going to do.

I was excited to see Traci in class and talk to her about my plan because I was going to need her help that afternoon after soccer. But when I walked into the English classroom and saw the look on her face, I knew she had something to tell me first.

"What's the matter?" I asked her.

She looked furious and flushed. Her mouth was set, and her eyes were wide-open.

"You are not. Going. To. Believe it," she said. "I promise you won't."

"Did something happen with Felicia?" I asked. "You didn't talk to her, did you?"

"Oh, I talked to her. I talked to her, all right. She had some interesting news for me," she said.

"What? Tell me!"

"She said . . . are you ready? She said she was *not going to do Healing Paws anymore.*"

My mouth dropped open. "*What?* You're joking. That has to be a joke! It's her *own father's animal shelter!*

She has to do it! We need her. Besides, she said she loved it, remember, just last week?" I said.

All of a sudden I realized that I was really upset and I felt like crying. And that made me even more mad.

Healing Paws was something sacred with us. I don't even like animals that much, but even I could see that it was amazing to give those kids a chance to be happy for a little while. And we really did need Felicia for the program to go well. She was the one who knew the most about the animals and the way they needed to be transported.

She also helped decide which animals would be the best ones for the kids. She knew what the animals were like because she lived with them.

"It's like she's gone completely crazy," I said. "What did she say?"

"She said that she spends enough time with the animals already and that we didn't really need her because we had Penny helping, and now Dave is helping, too."

"This is absolutely the final straw, Traci."

"But what can we do?" Traci sighed and shook her head.

"We can get back at her," I said. "And we'll start this afternoon after soccer."

chapter
ELEVEN

From Arielle's diary

REVENGE PLAN

Goal: to undermine Felicia's self-confidence, which she would not have if it weren't for me.

Tactics:

1. Remind Felicia that I am the most popular sixth grader, not her, by reasserting my place at the seventh-grade lunch table.

2. Take away one of the things that Felicia has gained as a result of my hard work remaking her appearance—Patrick (who was interested in me first, anyway).

3. Make Felicia uncomfortable by being as snotty as possible whenever I see her.

4. Look better and have a better presentation than Felicia at all times.

5. Get Traci and Amanda to join my team and stop being so sympathetic.

The plan was simple: I was going to steal Patrick away from Felicia. It was a perfect and easy operation, and it would strike Felicia right in the heart, like she had done to us.

Traci and I had another soccer practice that afternoon. We played really hard again in the cold wind. I was so excited about my plan that I didn't need to act like a barbarian, the way I had last practice.

"Nice work out there today, Arielle," Coach Talbot said to me as I came off the field.

Traci and I were both wiped out, but we had one thing left to do before we went home.

We had to begin Operation: Revenge.

"We have to go to the locker room through the gym," I told Traci.

"What do you mean?" she asked. "Why?"

"Because Operation Revenge begins right now," I said.

"Okay," Traci said. "Whatever. I just hope it doesn't take too long because I'm really tired."

I was hoping to catch Patrick in the gym at basketball practice, and now was a good time because I knew I looked good. My cheeks would be red from the wind, and my hair would be all windblown. It was a different look than he was used to seeing, and I knew he'd fall for it like all guys did.

Traci and I peeked in the gym door, and sure enough, basketball practice was still going on.

"Perfect," I said to Traci. "Now we have to go in and sit down and look like we're talking until they take a break."

"Okay," she said, and followed me into the gym.

We sat down on the bleachers and chatted about English class and some other dumb stuff while also talking about Patrick.

"Okay, don't look right now, but in a minute tell me if he's looking over here."

"They're all looking over here, Arielle. I'm sure they're wondering why we're sitting here."

"Just act like we're sitting here because this is a good place to sit and talk," I said. "Now we're just waiting for them to take a break and I'll go over and talk to Patrick."

"Just like that?" Traci asked.

"Yeah, just like that," I said. Some things just need to be done.

We talked for a while longer until the coach blew the whistle, and the guys went over to the bench to get drinks and grab towels to wipe the sweat off their faces.

I jumped up at this and said to Traci, "You wait here."

I went over to the crowd on the bench.

"Hey, you guys!" I said.

"Hey," some of them said.

I was careful not to look right at Patrick at first but instead at the guys standing right next to him on each side.

"Do you guys have a home game next week?"

"Yeah," someone said. "Against Rockwell on Thursday."

"I'm videotaping each sport for my media class, and I want to come to a good game. Are you going to win? Because I don't want footage of you losing." I said it flirtatiously, looking at Patrick for a second and then looking away, like I was shy.

"Yeah! We're gonna win. Of course we'll win!" They all started shouting.

"Okay, then, thanks. I'll see you on Thursday," I said, and turned to walk away. But then I turned right back and talked directly to Patrick. "Oh . . . what time is the game?" I looked right at him without blinking.

"Uh, I think it's, um, uh, at three-thirty," he stammered.

SCORE! I got him.

"Okay," I said right to him again. "I guess I'll see you then."

And I turned and walked away, sure that his eyes were following me back to the bleachers.

"Is he looking at me?" I asked as I walked up to Traci.

"Totally. You are a master. You're unbelievable. You had those guys eating out of the palm of your hand in three sentences," she said, looking amazed.

"Okay. Phase one: complete," I said. "Let's hit the showers!"

"What's next? Traci asked as we walked to the locker room.

"Oh, wait and see. It's going to be good."

*　　　*　　　*

I dressed for success the next day with a short black skirt, my favorite purple sweater, and heels. I was going to turn up the heat on the revenge plan, and I had to look good.

I knew Patrick had earth science with Ms. Carrington before lunch, and so I waited outside the classroom and tried to look casual.

When the bell rang and kids started coming out, I made it look like an accident that I was running into him in the hall.

"Hey, aren't you a famous basketball player?" I asked him as he walked by, falling into step with him.

He laughed. "Yeah, I play forward for the Lakers," he said.

Pretty funny, I thought.

"Going to lunch?" I asked him.

"Yup," he answered.

I *hate* it when people say yup.

I tried to walk slowly toward the lunchroom because I wanted to make sure Felicia was already there when we made our entrance.

When we finally arrived, I asked Patrick what his favorite NBA teams were so he'd be talking to me as we walked to the lunch line.

As he answered me, I made a big show of looking up at him as he answered, like I was fascinated by what he was saying.

And then I got in the hot lunch line, even though I

had a perfectly good lunch in my bag. Honestly, the sacrifices I was making for revenge!

We got trays of food, and as we came back into the lunchroom, I pretended to laugh loudly at what he was saying, even though what he was saying was, "This Jell-O looks like it's about three years old."

"Where are you sitting?" I asked him, stopping right in the middle of the room for all to see.

"With you, I hope," he replied.

I cringed inside. This guy was really not my type, and I really hate it when guys say cheesy romantic things.

All for a higher cause, I said to myself.

"Should we go and take a seat by the window?" I asked him. "Then we can talk."

"Yeah, sure. Let's do it!" he said.

Let's do it? Where were we, on the basketball court? This guy was the farthest thing from smooth. I sure hoped Felicia was watching and I wasn't going through all of this for nothing.

I looked all around the lunchroom quickly as we walked to the table.

I finally spotted Felicia. She was sitting with the seventh graders at their regular table. She hadn't seen us yet because I knew she would be looking over if she had. But I knew for sure that somebody from that table would see us soon and point us out to her.

I vowed not to look her way again.

Traci, Dave, Amanda, and Ryan were all sitting nearby

at our regular table. I caught Traci's eye and waved at her. She smiled and waved back, and the whole table turned around.

Patrick and I sat down by the window at a table all to ourselves and made small talk.

I tried to pay attention while he talked about himself, acting like I was fascinated. I leaned in to hear what he was saying, and I laughed out loud every time he said anything even remotely funny.

What a major ego boost this guy's getting, I thought.

"I'm so happy to be hanging out with you, Arielle," he said.

"Hmmm?" I smiled at him. "Oh, me too! We should have done this a long time ago."

"Well, I was wondering if you might like to go out sometime?" he asked. I couldn't believe how nervous he looked. He really liked me, I could see, but he was so not my type. *So* not my type.

"Oh, go out? Sure! I'd love to," I told him.

"Great. Well, you know Serena, right? She's having a party after the fall choral concert. I was wondering if you might like to go as my date."

"Oh, Patrick, that would be great!"

It was great, too. In one fell swoop I got massive revenge *and* an invitation to Serena's party.

I figured I could lose Patrick as soon as I got to the party.

This would be the ultimate revenge on Felicia.

Patrick and I got up to leave, and for the first time all lunch period, I looked over at Felicia. When I turned around, she was staring right at us with a terrible expression on her face. She was obviously angry and very upset.

I looked from her right to Patrick and said, with a big warm smile, "It was fun talking to you, Patrick—see you later."

I couldn't think of a better way to teach Felicia a lesson, and the lesson was, *Don't mess with the best.*

Amanda, Traci, Dave, and I met at the pizza parlor the next morning to take the bus out to Felicia's for Healing Paws.

Every week, on Healing Paws days, we went out to the shelter to load the animals into the trailer, and then we would drive with Mr. Fiol to the hospital.

"Hi, girls, hi, Dave," Penny said as we arrived. It was obvious that she felt a little awkward about Felicia not being there.

It was weird. The last time we had seen Penny was the night of the makeover. The night everything had changed. It seemed like such a long time ago.

"I wonder where Felicia is," Amanda whispered to me.

"I know. This is weird," I said.

But we didn't discuss it. Nobody mentioned Felicia's absence, even though I was sure Mr. Fiol and Penny were confused. Pretty soon there was so much work to do that there wasn't time to talk about it, anyway.

First we needed to pick which animals we were going to take with us.

We had the sign-up list with the kids' requests on it, and we figured we'd better take a bunch of extra animals, too, in case there were new kids or kids who didn't know to sign up.

Mr. Fiol had special wipes to clean the animals with, so we didn't have to give them each a bath before we went. He handed me a box and asked me to go and clean the kittens. There was a litter of six kittens about eight weeks old that we were going to bring, and I got to work wiping them down.

They were so adorable that it was hard to avoid squeezing them too hard when I picked them up.

They were in a box in the barn with their mom. Whenever I picked one up, it would meow in a tiny voice as I cleaned its fur with the cloth. The mom would look up at me suspiciously as I held it, but she'd quickly get distracted by the rest of the babies trying to play with her tail.

After I cleaned each one, I loaded it into the cage we would carry them in.

Finally, I cleaned the mom and put her in the cage.

Mr. Fiol had told me to only load the kittens, but I felt so bad for the mom sitting there wondering where her babies were that I decided we would have to bring her, too.

I brought the cage of kittens out to the yard and held them up for everyone to see.

"Awwwww!" everybody said.

"AAAAA-choo!" Dave sneezed.

Everyone said "bless you" at once, and we all laughed.

Amanda had been cleaning three beagle puppies, and she came out with them in her arms. They were squirming and whining, and they were the cutest things ever. She put them on the floor of the trailer to just run around, and they quickly discovered the cage full of kittens.

They went over and yelped at the kittens and stuck their noses between the bars of the cage.

The mom hissed at them, but the kittens just went up to them and started batting at their noses, which made them bark more.

I couldn't wait to get to the hospital so the kids could see all this.

Then Mr. Fiol said, "Okay, everybody, I have a surprise for you! Wait until you see this!"

He went into the chicken coop and came out with a box held high over his head.

"Ready, everyone? Come over and gather round."

I could hear some chirping, and when he lowered the box, we could see that the eggs he was incubating had hatched, and inside were about a hundred fuzzy fluffy yellow chicks. They were peeping these tiny peeps and crawling all over each other.

They were so cute, my heart just about broke.

I couldn't wait to show them to Phillip, the little boy with the broken leg. He loved tiny little animals like this.

Finally, all the animals were loaded into the trailer, and we piled into the van to go to the hospital.

It was funny, I had stopped thinking about Felicia for a few minutes while we were getting the animals ready, but during the ride to the hospital I had a chance to think about it. I realized that I didn't feel angry at the moment—I just felt sad for Felicia that she was missing all this.

I walked into Phillip's room with a tiny chick in my hand but held behind my back so he couldn't see it.

"*Hi!* I'm so happy you're here!" he shouted when he saw me.

While most of the kids went to the recreation room to play with the animals, Phillip had just had a major operation on his leg and it was in traction, so he couldn't leave his hospital bed.

"Can you guess what I have behind my back?" I asked him. Phillip was about six years old and really sweet.

"Um, a gerbil?"

"Nooooo!"

"A turtle?"

"Nooooo!"

He listened for a minute and heard the peeping.

"A chick?"

"Yes!" I said, and brought it out from behind my back.

I handed the tiny yellow ball of fluff to him, and he beamed.

"Oh, look how soft it is!" He held it up to his cheek to feel its soft feathers.

"Do you like it?" I asked.

"I love it. Look at its little beak. And it's telling me PEEP, PEEP, PEEP!"

He held it gently in his hand, and I told him what a great job he was doing because baby chicks are so fragile.

"Do you want to hold another one?" I asked him.

"There's more? *Yes*, I want to hold another one!"

There were about ninety-nine more, actually.

"I'll be right back," I said.

I went to the recreation room, where all the other kids were gathered.

The puppies were running around, barking at the kittens and the chicks, and the kittens were all being held by smiling kids.

I took about ten more chicks in the crook of my arm and went back to Phillip's room.

"Wow!" he said as I walked in with them.

I piled the chicks on his bed, and he picked each one up and named it.

"Hi, Rick, hi, Nick, hi, Mick, hi, Dick. Hi, Bill, hi, Jill, hi, Will, hi, Phil."

He sat and played with them happily. I couldn't help thinking about Felicia again and how much she would have enjoyed this.

chapter
TWELVE

Lyrics to Shauna Ferris's song "You Owe Me, Baby"

I gave you everything I had,
You should just love me and be glad,
Why do you have to make me mad?
Oh, oh, oh, you owe me, baby.
You got the nerve to walk away,
Don't think I'm begging you to stay,
You know I'm gonna make you pay,
Oh, oh, oh, you owe me, baby.
Yeah, you owe me one . . . two . . . three,
Nothing in this life is free.
You're gonna pay now—can't you see?
You . . . owe . . . me.

I made sure to get to lunch early on Monday so that I could sit at the seventh-grade table with Patrick.

My plan was to be in Felicia's face with Patrick as much as possible.

I waited for him outside his earth science class again right before lunch and walked him to the lunchroom for a repeat performance of Friday.

"Let's sit at your table today," I said as we walked in.

"Okeydokey!" he said. I really hate it when people say okeydokey.

"I have my own lunch today, so I'll go sit down and save you a seat," I told him.

"Okay, Arielle. See you in a minute," he said, thankfully skipping the okeydokey this time.

I went over to the table, which was about halfway full, and picked a seat, putting my bag down next to me to save a seat for Patrick.

"Hey, Arielle," Serena said as she sat down next to me on the other side. "How's it going?" *Perfect!* I would have Patrick on one side and Serena on the other when Felicia came up.

"Great, Serena. How are you?"

Serena took out her lunch and started talking about her party at the end of the week. She asked me if I wanted to come, and I didn't tell her I already had plans to go with Patrick. I didn't want it to look like I was trying to steal Patrick from Felicia, although that's exactly what I was doing.

"This looks more like dog food than human food," I heard Patrick say as he sat down. "Heh, heh, heh." He laughed at his own joke.

Then I saw Felicia coming in the door of the lunchroom, so I threw back my head and laughed like he just said the funniest thing I'd ever heard.

"So tell me a little about how you started playing basketball," I said to him. Then I cocked my head and listened intently as he told me how he was good at basketball because he was tall. What a story.

I could see Felicia out of the corner of my eye, trying to decide where to sit. I looked right at her for a minute, and she looked right at me with a hurt, sort of angry expression on her face.

Then she picked a seat at the end of the table, as far away from me and Patrick as she could get.

"So what's that you're eating?" Patrick asked me.

"Oh, this? This is sushi," I told him.

"Sushi? I've heard of that. That's like raw fish, right?" he asked.

"Yes, but this has no raw fish in it. It's just vegetables. Raw fish wouldn't keep in my locker until lunch," I said.

"Oh yeah. I guess that makes sense," he said.

I noticed that Felicia wasn't greeted with the fanfare that she had been for the last couple of weeks.

I guess the novelty of her new look was wearing off.

I mean, everybody was friendly to her, but they were just carrying on as if she was a regular part of the group. Serena wasn't saving her a seat anymore, and the conversation didn't totally revolve around her.

"So what did you do this weekend?" Serena asked me.

"Traci and Amanda and I did the Healing Paws program at the hospital. It was *so* much fun," I said.

"Healing Paws? What's that?" Serena asked.

"Oh, actually, it's a program with Felicia's dad's animal shelter." I shot a look at Felicia, who looked kind of uncomfortable. "I'm surprised she didn't tell you. We bring puppies and kittens and other animals to the hospital to play with the kids there."

"Wow," she said, "that sounds amazing! I'd love to do that sometime."

"Well, actually, it just so happens that we're looking for a new volunteer," I said.

"Maybe I can get your phone number and you can tell me more about it." Serena pulled out her cell phone and prepared to add me to the number listing. "You can decide whether you think I'd be a good volunteer."

"Okay, great," I said, and gave her my number. Then I took out a pen and my address book from my bag. I handed them to Serena, and she wrote her name and number in the book.

"I love animals, and I love kids, too, so maybe it would work out," she said.

I glanced over at Felicia and saw that she was having trouble keeping from looking upset. She was far enough away that she couldn't hear our conversation, but she didn't need to hear the whole thing to tell that Serena and Patrick were having a great time talking to me.

She was chewing her fingernails and looking at her tray and generally looking unhappy. If we were still friends, I would have reminded her that she was breaking all the rules of presentation.

My plan was working perfectly. I was taking away from Felicia all the things that I had given her. She didn't deserve them.

"I'm really looking forward to Serena's party, Patrick," I said.

"Oh, me too, Arielle," he said, and gave me a big goofy smile.

"I'll see you all later," I said, packing up my lunch. I had to talk to Traci and Amanda and tell them how it went.

Besides, later that afternoon I had another Operation: Revenge mission planned, and I needed their help.

Dave and Ryan were deep in conversation about some video game, so I could talk to the girls privately.

"I can't believe how unhappy Felicia looks, Arielle," Amanda said. "You really got to her. I almost feel sorry for her."

"Don't," I told her. "She doesn't deserve it."

"I guess not, but I feel kind of bad for her, too," Traci said.

Jeez. Trust these girls to go soft on me when the going got tough.

"Do you think she felt sorry for us when we felt so bad because she ignored us like we were just a bunch of passing acquaintances?"

Traci frowned. "No, she really didn't, did she?"

"No! She didn't. Now, listen. We have something to do this afternoon," I said.

"What?" Traci asked.

"Practice for the chorus concert is at three-thirty. We're going to go and sit through it. We can say we're there to listen to Ryan."

"Huh? Are you girls talking about me?" Ryan said, perking up at the sound of his name.

"Yes," I said. "It's all about you. We were saying that you were the handsomest boy at Wonder Lake Middle School," I joked.

"Hey, what about me?" Dave asked with a laugh.

"You're the smartest," Amanda said, and put her arm around him, smiling.

"I'd rather be the best-looking," he said.

"Boys, go back to your conversation," Traci said. "We're talking here."

"Okay. No problem. Anyway, Dave, what I was saying about that level—" Ryan began to drone on again.

"So listen, why are we going to concert practice?" Amanda asked.

"We're going to go and make Felicia feel uncomfortable," I explained. "She can ignore us, but we're not going to go away. And she'll just have to live with that."

"Hmmm, okay. That sounds good. And actually, I wait for my mom in the auditorium all the time when she has something after school. It'll just look like you guys are waiting with me," Traci said.

"Great!" I said. "So we'll see you then. Three-thirty in the auditorium. The second phase of Operation Revenge!"

The houselights were on in the auditorium when I showed up. I was a little late because I had stopped to talk to Patrick, who I ran into in the hall. It was important for me to keep our relationship solid at this point.

"Arielle!" Ryan said as he spotted me walking in. "Wow, all you girls are here because you love the sound of my voice so much that one concert is not enough?"

"Yes, Ryan. We're all here because of you," Traci said, smiling at him.

It seemed like Traci and Ryan used to be a lot funnier before they got to liking each other so much. Maybe it was because they felt like they didn't have to impress each another anymore.

I sat down in the row next to Amanda and looked around.

"Look over there," Amanda said, pointing low. "There she is. She keeps looking over here at us."

"Oh, yeah," I said, spotting her. "She doesn't look very happy."

"No, not at all. You know, I'm not so sure this is a good idea," Amanda said.

"Amanda, please try to keep in mind what *she* did to *us*, will you? You are *so* too nice."

"Okay," she said. "You're right. I'm sorry."

We took our books and pretended to do our

homework, for Ms. McClintic's sake, and we clapped for Ryan when he was done.

"Okay, Felicia!" Ms. McClintic called when the applause had faded. "Are you here? Come on up and let's hear how you're sounding."

Felicia looked nervous as she walked up to the stage. She looked at the ground and climbed the steps of the stage with her fingernail in her mouth.

"Have you been working on that section we talked about, hon?" Ms. McClintic asked.

"Um, yes, I have," she said in a small voice.

"Okay, then, let's give it a try," Ms. McClintic said, and started to play.

Felicia started to sing, but she sounded *completely* different from when she had sung at the audition. Her voice was wavery and unsure and kept cracking at the high parts. She sounded terrible!

Her confidence was gone.

"Honey, do you feel okay?" Ms. McClintic asked.

She just nodded.

"Would you like to start over and try again?"

"Yeah, why don't I?" Felicia said.

She took a deep breath and tried to smile. But then I saw her glance over at us just as she started singing.

Again just the worst noise ever came out of her mouth. Her confidence was totally gone, and with it her beautiful singing voice.

She got through the song and even improved a little at the end, but overall, she was just terrible.

Ms. McClintic looked worried, and Felicia looked like she was about to cry.

"You know what, let's just take a break for today, and you and I will get together tomorrow and practice before the concert," Ms. McClintic said. "I know you can do it beautifully. You're just nervous, and we can work on that, okay?"

"Okay. Sorry, Ms. McClintic," she said.

"No big deal, honey! We'll figure it out," Traci's mom said.

Felicia practically shuffled off the stage and took a seat.

She turned her face away from us, and after a minute I saw her shoulders shaking. I realized with a start that she was crying.

"Let's go, you guys," I said to Traci and Amanda. I wanted to get them out of there before they saw Felicia crying.

We went out the back door of the auditorium.

"I feel pretty bad for her," Traci said as the door swung shut behind us.

"Yeah, me too. That was really awful," Amanda said.

The fact was, I felt pretty bad, too. I mean, I wanted revenge, but now that I sort of had it, it made me feel terrible to see Felicia so sad.

Nobody should have to sit alone and cry like that.

"Let's talk about it tonight," I said. "I have to get home, but I'll call you guys three-way at seven, okay?"

"Okay, talk to you then," they said.

By the time seven o'clock rolled around, I had stopped feeling sorry for Felicia. When I thought about how sad it was that she was crying, I remembered the times that she had made *me* cry in the last couple of weeks. And I hadn't seen her caring about me then.

So when I called Traci and Amanda, I knew I was ready to convince them that we should continue with Operation Revenge.

A three-way call is confusing because you can't always tell who's talking, but it was necessary tonight.

"Listen, I know you both feel bad about what happened today in the auditorium, but I think we have to be firm about this," I said once I had the two of them on the phone.

"I knew you were going to say that, Arielle. I was going to say that I think we should call her," Amanda said.

"No way! We are *not* calling her unless it's to tell her what a jerk she is," I objected.

Traci spoke. "I'm somewhere in the middle. I don't want to call her, but I don't want her to feel so bad, either. Arielle, I know she was mean to us, but I'm not the kind of person who can just let my friends feel bad."

"That's the problem, Traci. You're still thinking of

Felicia as your friend. Has she been a friend to you in any way in the last two weeks?"

"No, I guess not," Traci said.

"But, Arielle, everybody makes mistakes. Think of all the things we've forgiven *you* for," Amanda said.

I didn't have an answer for that. It was true that they had forgiven me for some pretty bad stuff. But they did make me suffer for a while over it, too.

"Well, maybe that's it. How about this: I'm not saying we'll never be friends with Felicia again. I'm just saying we can't forgive her at the drop of the first tear."

"That's true, I guess," Amanda said. "I mean, she can't just dump on us and expect that we'll be there for her as soon as she misses us."

"Exactly," I said.

"It's not like she called and apologized," Traci said.

"No, she hasn't apologized at all, has she?" Amanda said. "If she said she was sorry, that might be a different story."

"You know, if she said she was sorry, I think I'd have a hard time *not* forgiving her," Traci said.

"Yeah, me too," Amanda said.

"So maybe we should make that our decision," I suggested. "We'll wait to hear an apology from her, and then we'll take her back as a friend."

"Sounds good to me," Traci said. "I feel bad for her, but an apology is the least we deserve."

"Okay, then. We wait for Felicia to say she's sorry," I said.

I know Felicia pretty well, and if there was one thing I was sure about, it was that Felicia would almost never apologize. She was just one of those people who had a really hard time saying she was sorry.

"So are you actually going to go out with Patrick, Arielle?" Amanda asked.

"I don't know. I'm not attracted to him at all, but it sure is having the effect on Felicia that we wanted," I said.

"But do you think it's fair to him to pretend you like him when you really don't?" Traci asked me.

"It makes him feel good to think I like him. It's a total ego boost for him that I listen to his stories and laugh at his jokes every day at lunch," I said.

"But that's fake," Amanda said.

"He doesn't know that," I replied. "And he never has to."

"He'll figure it out when you dump him when you're through using him to make Felicia feel bad," Traci said.

"I'll let him down gently. Don't worry, girls," I said.

"If you say so," Amanda said.

"So now that that's settled, can we talk a little bit about surface tension on water?" I asked, pulling out my science notebook. "You guys did *not* explain it to me right."

chapter
THIRTEEN

Note on Davises' bulletin board to Arielle from her mom

Ari—

We won't be home until after your bedtime tonight— we have a bar association event. Use the credit card to buy yourself dinner and go shopping if you want. Also, Dad and I decided that if you really want voice lessons, you can have them. Let's try to spend some time together this weekend.

Love, Mom

It didn't surprise me in the least that Felicia didn't apologize the next day or any other day that week. She did start changing the way she was acting, though.

For one thing, she stopped eating with the seventh-grade table every day. One day I saw her eating with a group of orchestra kids. Then we saw her eating by herself, quickly, and getting up and leaving. And then one day she wasn't at lunch at all.

She was still blowing out her hair and wearing the same makeup as before, but the clothes she was wearing were a little less flashy each day.

Then on Friday morning, the day of the fall concert, we saw her at her locker, and she did the most shocking thing!

She walked over and said hello to us.

She looked nervous. "Hi, you guys."

"Hi, Felicia," Amanda said, in a not friendly but not rude voice.

"Hey," Traci said.

I didn't say anything at all, but I didn't walk away, either, like I was tempted to do. That was as nice as I was going to be.

"How's it going?" she asked.

And that's when I noticed it. Her hair was curly! She hadn't blow-dried it straight that morning. She was abandoning the makeover, bit by bit.

I wondered if that was her way of apologizing.

"It's going okay," I said. "How's it going with you?"

Traci and Amanda looked at me, shocked. They obviously couldn't believe that I was speaking to Felicia.

"Everything's okay," Felicia said, slinging her backpack over her shoulder. "Well, I'd better get to homeroom. I'll see you guys later. Bye."

And she walked away. Maybe she left so fast because she was afraid somebody was going to say something mean to her.

"Did you see that, guys?" I asked Traci and Amanda.

"See what, Arielle?" Amanda asked.

"Felicia had her hair natural just now. She's dropped one of the main parts of the makeover. And she had barely any makeup on, and she was wearing almost normal clothes," I said.

"Yeah, she seems like she's really depressed," Traci said. "But she still didn't apologize."

"No, listen. Felicia *never* says she's sorry. She's really bad at it. But I think this is her way of apologizing to us. By going back to her normal look, she's saying she wants to go back to the way things were!"

"Look who's going soft on us." Amanda shook her head in disbelief. "I think it's more likely that she woke up late this morning and didn't have time to spend an hour on her hair."

"No, I'm telling you. I know Felicia," I said. "I'm not saying I'm forgiving her, I'm just saying she's making an effort."

"Okay, if you say so," Traci said dubiously.

But I could tell that both of them *wanted* to believe me.

I was still really mad at Felicia, and I still wanted my revenge, but part of me really hoped we could all be friends again.

"Well, my mom says she's been working like crazy to get Felicia ready for the concert," Traci said. "She says that it seems like Felicia's lost her confidence and hasn't been able to sing the song as well as she sang it at the audition."

At the mention of the Shauna song I felt myself start to get angry again. By all rights *I* should be the one performing in that concert tonight.

"That's what she gets for stealing the song from me. Hopefully she'll sound awful tonight and everyone will know what she's really like—a loser," I said.

"Jeez, Arielle. You were just so happy that she was apologizing to us," Traci said.

"Yeah, I know. Then I remembered that she's actually a snake," I said, but a tiny part of me wasn't as angry as all that.

I arrived really early in the auditorium for the concert that night, and I went straight up to the front row to save seats for Amanda and Traci.

I couldn't decide if I wanted to sit in the front row because I wanted Felicia to see us and feel uncomfortable or because I wanted her to know that we were rooting for her.

It was a little bit of both, I finally decided.

Traci showed up first and sat down next to me.

"My mom is a wreck, she's so nervous," she said. "She's really worried about Felicia's solo. It's the last song of the concert, and she says Felicia never really got her groove back."

I shrugged. "Your mom should have given me the solo. My groove never goes anywhere. I keep it right here with me at all times," and I did a little funky dancing in my seat to show her.

She cracked up.

"Anyway, she said she was thinking about changing the order of the songs so that Felicia wasn't last, but they had already printed up the programs," Traci added.

"Bummer," I said.

"Hey, there's Amanda and Dave." She waved them over.

"Mom's freaking out," Dave said as he sat down. "I can't believe how nervous she gets."

"I know. Remember how she made me practice for hours on end before the orchestra competition? Thank goodness I'm not in this concert," Traci said.

"Have you seen Felicia?" Amanda asked. "I just saw her on her way backstage. She's got her hair done and a skimpy little Shauna outfit on. So much for your apology theory, Arielle."

But I knew Amanda was wrong. After all, it was a concert. You kind of *had* to get dressed up.

The concert started out fine. Ryan's performance was fantastic, and we all clapped like crazy for him, but I think all of us were on the edge of our seats, waiting for Felicia.

Part of me was glad I didn't have to perform that night because I could feel how nervous I'd be if it was me. I was sure Felicia must be freaking out.

Finally, the applause for the barbershop quartet died down, and it was time for Felicia's solo.

They brought the lights down low for her entrance, and Ms. McClintic announced, "Ladies and gentlemen, here's Felicia Fiol, singing 'You Owe Me, Baby,' by Shauny Ferris!"

"Oh my God, she said 'Shauny' instead of 'Shauna'!" Traci hissed over the applause.

I shook my head. "Unbelievable."

Serena and her friends were a couple of rows back, and we could hear them cheering like crazy. *They'd better cheer,* I thought. *If this doesn't go well, it will have been all their fault. It was their idea in the first place.*

That's when I realized how nervous I was for Felicia and how much I really *did* hope she'd do well.

There was a special spotlight for this song, and the crowd hushed as Felicia came out and stood by the microphone.

She looked really pretty in her Shauna getup but terrified.

The music started, and Felicia's cue came, but Felicia didn't sing.

Ms. McClintic looked up at her, smiled an encouraging smile, and repeated the line of music over again. This time Felicia opened her mouth, but no sound came out. Her eyes opened really wide. She really looked like a deer caught in the headlights.

"Oh, *no!*" I whispered to Amanda and Traci.

Ms. McClintic kept playing and smiling, obviously hoping for the best, but it was clear that Felicia didn't remember how the song started or something.

I had to do something! So in a loud whisper I shouted the first line of the song to her.

This seemed to snap her out of her frozen state. She looked at me, sort of stunned, then started to sing the line I gave her. I could see Ms. McClintic let out a sigh of relief.

Felicia's voice was tiny and squeaky. When the line ended, she stopped dead with the music still playing. She was completely frozen.

So I called out the next line.

When the music hit the right place, she sang out that line, too. And then she stopped again.

I called out the next line. I had to get her through this. But instead of singing it, Felicia looked over at me. For the first time she seemed to come out of her frightened daze, and she actually looked kind of grateful. Then she did something that totally shocked me. She came over to the edge of the stage and reached out her hand to me, as if to pull me up there with her.

Ms. McClintic, obviously hoping for a miracle, just kept playing the song.

I looked over at Traci and Amanda, and they were both smiling and nodding, so I jumped up. I grabbed Felicia's hand, and she pulled me up onto the stage with one hard yank. She was smiling now, like a million dollars.

It was hot, and the lights were blinding up there. It was like a whole different world.

We went to the microphone together, and as if we'd practiced it forever, we started singing the song together.

Our voices sounded great together, and I knew it and she knew it. It was like we both had instant confidence and because our voices covered for each other.

I started dancing a little while still singing into the microphone and then so did Felicia. I could hear the crowd cheering us, and that made me dance even a little bit harder, and pretty soon we were jumping all over the place.

Felicia took the mike off its stand and we sang into it, and then took a bar to do some dance moves, and then went back to the mike to sing some more. Felicia was laughing, and I couldn't help giggling a little, too. This was *so* much more fun than singing it alone would have been. The audience was totally loving it, laughing and cheering for our crazy dance moves. This was one of the best feelings I'd ever had.

For the last lines of the song Felicia put the microphone back on its stand, and we stood next to it and sang quietly.

Oh yeah, you owe me,
But you're my friend,
So I will hold you
Until the end,

And though there's nothing
In life for free,
What's more important
Is you and meeeeee.

We threw our arms around each other at the very end, and as we finished, the crowd went wild.

They clapped for at least two straight minutes, and then Serena and her friends led a standing ovation. The entire auditorium was standing and clapping for us. I looked at Felicia, and she was smiling so wide, she almost looked like she might cry.

I looked over at Ms. McClintic, and she was standing at her piano bench, hands high in the air, clapping for us and beaming.

I turned and gave Felicia a hug, right up there in front of everybody.

Slowly the applause died down, and the lights came up and we came down from the stage to where Amanda and Traci and Ryan and Dave were waiting for us by our seats.

Traci was smiling so huge, and she threw her arms around us and hugged us as we walked up.

"You guys were incredible! I've never seen anything like it," she said.

"I'm so proud of you!" Amanda said. She gave Felicia a big hug. "I missed you so much, Felicia."

"I missed you guys, too," Felicia said, and she

burst into tears. "I was so awful to you guys. Thank you so much, Arielle!"

She turned and hugged me again.

Just then Ms. McClintic walked up to congratulate us.

"You girls were the absolute biggest hit of the show. And what great music you made. Thank you, Arielle!"

"Oh, I had a great time, Ms. McClintic. I really want to join chorus now!"

The auditorium started to empty out, and after a bunch of people came over to tell us how great we were, the four of us—Amanda, Traci, Felicia, and me—were left standing there by ourselves.

"Listen, you guys, I don't know quite how to say this, but I do feel bad about the way I acted. . . . I just was so embarrassed, and I acted like such a jerk. But I didn't know how to tell you or what to say, and so I just wandered around miserable. . . ." Felicia trailed off.

"Um, Felicia? Do you mean to say you're sorry?" I asked her, smiling.

"Yes! That! I'm that. I'm . . . sorry. I'm so sorry, you guys."

Amanda and Traci laughed. "We forgive you, Felicia," Traci said.

"I guess you were right, Arielle," Amanda said.

"Right about what?" Felicia asked.

"Arielle told us you have a hard time saying you're sorry," Amanda told her. "I couldn't help but notice that she's right. But it doesn't matter. I'm just so glad to have you back."

Amanda put her arm around Felicia, and Felicia looked like she was going to cry again from relief.

"Thank goodness all this is over," she said. "I've been so unhappy for two weeks and so nervous about this stupid concert, I thought I would die."

Dave and Ryan came over and congratulated us again. "Everybody's talking about you," Dave said. "Eric Rich just asked me what your name was, Arielle."

"He did? Oh, my God!" I gasped.

"We told him it was Martha Birnbaum," Ryan said. "And that you were a visiting special ed student."

"Oh, thanks a lot, Ryan!" I said, laughing.

"Hey, do you want to ask if we can all go out for pizza?" Dave asked.

"Yeah, why not? I'll go find my dad and see if he'll drive us in the van," Felicia said. "I have to find him, anyway, so he can tell me how great I was!"

And that's when it hit me: Serena's party. Patrick. Oh, no. Double oh, no. Felicia was finally back with us and we were all feeling great, and I had the worst betrayal of all in the works.

Patrick was waiting for me on the front steps, and his mom was going to drive us to Serena's party.

Oh, what a huge mistake! I moaned. I felt awful, and I couldn't figure out what to do.

But then, just like that, I had an idea.

chapter
FOURTEEN

Wonder Lake Pizza order pad

ORDER Table 5: One large Sicilian, half anchovies, half sausage; one large regular, half pepperoni, half meatballs; one large white, easy on the cheese, with chicken and basil. Four diet Cokes, two Cokes.

I ran to the front steps to find Patrick. I was really late to meet him because I had forgotten all about him!

"Hey!" he said as I walked up. "You were so great up there. What a big surprise!"

"Thanks, Patrick. I'm so sorry I'm late."

"It's no problem. I know you had to sign autographs for all your fans," he said with a grin.

Now, *that* was pretty funny. Maybe he wasn't so bad after all.

"You know," he said, "Felicia was amazing, too. I didn't know she had such a great voice."

Okay, I thought. *Now we're getting somewhere. That's the idea.*

"So are you ready to go?" he asked.

"Actually," I said with a smile, "I was wondering if you'd mind if we changed our plans a little?"

"No, whatever you want to do," he said. "I'm not really in the mood to go to a party, anyway."

"Well, I was going to meet my friends at the pizza parlor for some pizza and just to hang out. Will you come and join us?" I asked.

"Sure, that sounds great," he said.

"I have to go and do a couple of things first. Should we meet there in, say, half an hour?" I said.

"Okay, I'll see you there!"

I ran back inside the auditorium. Everybody was waiting for me.

"Where were you?" Amanda asked me.

"Signing autographs," I said, stealing Patrick's joke.

Mr. Fiol and Penny were there, waiting to take all of us in the van.

"Hey, you were terrific up there, Arielle," Felicia's dad said.

"I'll say!" Penny added. "Talk about teamwork. You two were spectacular."

"Thanks a lot," I said, smiling. I was so happy. I just hoped I could pull off my plan.

As we walked to the van, I thought about the fact that while revenge felt pretty good, it was in a mean way. Forgiveness felt a whole lot better.

*　　　*　　　*

When we got to the pizza parlor, Penny and Mr. Fiol went off and sat in a booth on the other side of the restaurant to give us our space.

"Let's push these two tables together," Dave said.

"No, we have to sit in a booth," I announced.

"But we won't all fit in a booth," Traci protested.

"That's okay—we'll just all squeeze in," I said.

"But why would we do that?" Dave asked.

"What it this? McClintic twenty questions night?" I said. "Let's just sit down."

"Okay, then, if it means so much to you." Dave shrugged.

We all had to cram in to fit in the booth, so I got a chair and put it on the end for Felicia. "Hey, Felicia, here's a chair for you."

"You want me to sit here, Arielle? Why?" she asked.

"Just because," I said. "No reason. Oh, by the way, we may be expecting someone else."

"Who?" Traci demanded. "And if we're expecting someone else, why the heck are we crammed into this tiny booth?"

But I guess Amanda had figured it out because she kicked Traci under the table.

"So tell us the truth, you two," Dave said. "You had that planned out all along, didn't you?" He grinned at me and Felicia.

"What!" Felicia laughed. "No! Not at all. I really

was petrified and frozen up there, and thank goodness Arielle came to my rescue."

"But you guys had obviously rehearsed it and everything just in case or something, right?" Ryan said.

"No, we never did," I said.

"I *so* don't believe you," Ryan said.

"But we weren't even speaking to each other before the concert," Felicia pointed out. "How could we have rehearsed?"

"This is true," Dave said. "Well, anyway, you'd have to be pretty good friends and know each other pretty well to pull off something like that."

"Yeah, I guess that's right, huh?" Felicia said, smiling at me.

"Sure is." I smiled back.

"Whew! What a night! I'm starving," said Ryan.

"You're always starving," Traci teased him.

"No kidding. So what kind are we going to get?" Ryan pulled out the menu and pointed to the toppings.

"I want anchovies with pineapple," Dave said.

"Well, I want olive oil and lemon," I said.

We traded outrageous flavors and laughed until tears came out of our eyes. Then Sal came to take our order and found that we had no idea what we wanted. He shook his head and walked off, giving us five minutes to decide.

It was so amazing to have all of us together again. I

was sitting next to Felicia, and we were telling jokes and laughing about the dumbest stuff, just like the old premakeover days.

Then suddenly the bell on the door dinged. We were the only ones in the place, so we all turned around to see who it was.

It was, of course, Patrick.

For a moment everybody froze, including Patrick, who seemed to sense everybody's surprise at seeing him.

Felicia turned to me with a look on her face like I'd just taken out a knife and stabbed her.

But I just kept smiling. She'd see.

"Hey, Patrick," I called. "Come on over. We just ordered, so you didn't miss anything."

"Oh, sorry, didn't you know? The pizzas came, and I ate them so fast that none of you even saw. Sorry about that," Ryan said.

It was a completely lame joke to try to cut the tension, and unfortunately, it didn't work. No one laughed.

But that didn't matter. It was going to work out fine. I just knew it. Or at least, I hoped.

Patrick crossed the length of the restaurant to get to us with everybody staring at him.

"Hey, does everybody know Patrick?" I said brightly, hoping to fill the air with cheerfulness. Of course everybody knew him.

"Hey, Patrick," Ryan said.

"Hi, Patrick, how are you?" Amanda said. She was

the only one who got what was going on, so she sounded cheery.

Felicia just stared at me, not saying anything.

"So we're out of room at this booth," I said. "Hey, Felicia, since you're on the end, do you want to start a new booth behind us with Patrick, and then when the others show up, they can join you?"

Suddenly, comprehension flashed on Felicia's face.

She smiled. "Sure! We can do that. Come on, Patrick."

They went and sat down together in the booth right behind us, and I took Felicia's place at the head of the table.

"Nice work, Ari," Traci said, looking happy to finally get what was going on.

Traci and Amanda were smiling at me, but Ryan and Dave looked like they were utterly baffled by Patrick's arrival and our maneuvering. But like typical guys, they didn't ask what was up. The pizza arrived and was more important than anything else.

"Give me a slice of each, would you," Ryan said, passing his plate to me.

I was the automatic server girl because I was at the head of the table.

"Patrick, Felicia, what do you guys want?" I called to the other booth.

They didn't answer but just kept on talking. It looked like they were in their own little world.

"Hey! Earth to table two! Are you guys eating or are you just here to chat?" I joked.

"Oh, sorry, Arielle!" Felicia said. She turned to me, and she was laughing and her eyes were so bright. She looked happy, and suddenly, I felt great. It really was a good feeling to be able to do things for your friends.

Maybe making people feel good is better than making people feel bad.

Patrick and Felicia seem to really be hitting it off, I thought.

That's when I noticed that I was the only one alone that night.

Felicia was with Patrick, Amanda was with Dave, Traci was with Ryan. Even Mr. Fiol was with Penny.

But for whatever reason, I felt so good that it didn't bother me at all.

Who knew, maybe Eric Rich would ask me out or maybe someone else. But for the moment it was fine to be on my own, with my friends.

chapter
FIFTEEN

From Arielle's diary

Nov. 16: Revenge plan is officially canceled.

New operation: BEING A BETTER PERSON.

Goal: Not hurting people you love.

<u>Tactics</u>:

1. Be more understanding when friends make mistakes—don't try to punish them, just try to talk to them.

2. Never mess with a guy a friend likes—you can have any guy you want, so there's no reason to pick one who's taken.

3. Don't get jealous when someone has something you want—just work slowly and patiently toward getting whatever it is for yourself.

4. Never make people feel bad about not being as pretty or as confident as you are—help friends feel more comfortable whenever possible.

A football game was playing on the TV in the pizza parlor, and after we were done eating, the guys started watching the game. After a while they got really into it, and it started to be really annoying.

Felicia was talking about how she felt up onstage before I came up.

"So I look out into the lights, and I can barely make out the audience, and I realize: I have no idea what the words—"

"YEAH! WHOA! You rule!" the boys suddenly screamed from right next to us.

"You guys! Felicia is talking. Why don't you go sit over there and watch the game?" Traci said, pointing to a table near the TV.

"Sorry we interrupted you," Patrick said to Felicia with a smile. I was starting to like him.

"That's okay." She smiled back at him.

The boys got up and moved. They ordered more sodas and settled in to watch the game, which gave the four of us some time to catch up.

I had mixed feelings about talking to Felicia about everything that had gone on in the past couple of weeks.

On the one hand, I was dying to know about what she had been up to . . . but on the other hand, I was really embarrassed by how I had acted.

She was probably embarrassed, too, though.

And then she seemed to read my mind.

"I want to tell you guys that I know how hard it must be to forgive me. I can't believe I acted that way," Felicia said.

"I feel the same," I told her. "I really wish I could take back some of the things I did. I wish the whole thing had never happened. It was my stupid idea to do the makeover in the first place, and look how it turned out."

"No, it wasn't your fault it turned out badly," she said. "It was mine. I should never have treated you guys the way I did."

"Well, I'm so glad it's all over," Amanda said.

"I noticed you were back to your regular self this morning at school. Are you going to stay that way?" Traci asked her.

"Well, I might dress up for special occasions, but I don't have the energy to spend so much time on my makeup and hair every single morning," Felicia said. "I don't know how you do it, Arielle."

"I've been doing it forever, so I've got it down to a science," I explained.

"But still," she said, "it was taking me an hour to do my hair and another hour to get dressed and do my makeup. I've been exhausted from getting up so early," she added with a laugh.

"But wasn't it fun getting to hang out with all those seventh graders?" Amanda asked.

"Yeah, I guess." Felicia shrugged. "I mean, it was

really fun to be noticed and to be the talk of that crowd for a while." She looked sheepishly at me. "I guess I've never really been popular before, and I liked how it felt."

I nodded. "Well, it *is* nice to get attention."

Felicia sighed. "The thing is, they're nice and everything, but after a while they just kind of lost interest in me. And when I really thought about it— like, what we talk about and what we all like to do—I like you guys much better," she said. "I'm glad I got to see what it felt like to be popular. But I'm even gladder that I have great friends like you."

I could feel my face getting a little red. "I was really jealous that they were paying so much attention to you, actually," I admitted.

"I know. I'm so sorry, Arielle. I felt so bad about it the whole time, and I missed you guys so much," Felicia said.

"You did? You acted like you didn't miss us at all," Traci said.

"Well, I was doing that thing Arielle taught me: Fake a smile until you actually feel happy. And then at least you'll look happy while you wait to feel better," Felicia said. "No offense, Arielle, but that was the worst advice anyone ever gave me!" She laughed.

I laughed, too. "You mean, you weren't really that happy?"

"I was happy for the first couple of days, when I was still hanging out with you guys, but I was pretty uncomfortable with all that makeup and new hair and clothes. I felt like a fake Felicia," she said.

"Well, you pulled it off," I said, smiling.

"Yeah, I guess, but I figured out that it *does* matter how you feel, not just how you look. You were so wrong about that."

"But you have to admit, looking good can make you feel great," I said.

"But don't you think I look good without all the bells and whistles? I mean, no one was screaming and running away from me when they saw me the old way. I didn't break any mirrors," Felicia said.

"Of course. You're totally beautiful," Amanda said.

"I really liked that all those boys were talking to me and everything, and then I started thinking about it, and I realized that they were only talking to me because they liked the way I looked," Felicia said.

"Well, that's not so wrong, is it?" I said.

"Not exactly, but I'd rather have real friends and a boyfriend who likes me for more reasons than that," she said.

"Yeah, I guess that makes sense," I had to admit.

Just then the boys watching the game let out a chorus of "Whooo! Yeah!" They were pounding on the table and yelling at the TV.

"Look at those guys. They are so into it," Traci said with a grin. "You know, I think Patrick is so cool, Felicia. Do you really like him?"

"Yeah, he seems like a really nice person. We've had some great conversations over the last couple of weeks. But when he started paying attention to you, Arielle, and ignoring me, I thought he was kind of a jerk," she said.

"That was totally my fault, Felicia," I said. "I'm so sorry. I was just trying to be mean and take him away from you. It was me that was putting moves on him, not the other way around."

"Really? Then you think he really does like me?" she asked.

"I do think so. He was saying how great you were in the concert tonight, actually, before we came here."

"Well, if he doesn't like the real me, with curly hair and no mascara, then he's going to have to take a hike." She nodded firmly.

"All right!" Traci said.

"You go, girl!" Amanda shouted.

We all laughed and sipped our sodas for a minute. It felt so good to talk about everything.

"You know what the worst day was, out of all of this?" Felicia asked.

"What?" I said.

"Last Saturday, when I missed Healing Paws. How was it?"

"Oh, it was great," Amanda said. "The kids were so cute, and we brought the newest kittens, you know, the really tiny ones?"

"And we also brought those baby chicks that finally hatched," I said.

"We really missed you," Traci said. "It felt like something was missing the entire day."

"I missed you guys, too," she said sadly.

"I don't understand how you could decide not to come, Felicia. What was the deal?" I asked in a nice voice. I wanted her to know I wasn't mad anymore.

"Well, Serena and her friends kept asking me to do stuff, and I felt like if I said no even once, they might never ask me again," she said. "I know that's crazy, but that's how I felt. That's why that day I was supposed to meet you guys after school," she said to Traci and Amanda, "I just went to the mall with Serena instead."

"Oh, yeah, that was a bummer," Amanda said.

"I felt so awful the entire time I was there that I thought I would throw up. Then I figured you guys hated me and I started avoiding you so I wouldn't have to face it."

"Great plan, Felicia," Amanda said sarcastically.

"We never hated you, Felicia," Traci said. "We could never hate you. We're best friends."

"You guys are the best," she said. "I'm so lucky to have friends like you."

The boys went crazy over the game again, whooping and screaming, and I saw Mr. Fiol get up to go and join them. Penny followed him.

"It's too bad there isn't some way to get her to

disappear," I said, gesturing toward Penny. "I mean, I know *you guys* like her"—I turned toward Amanda and Traci—"but still . . ."

"Yeah. I kind of agree," Felicia said frowning a little. "I mean, I definitely don't have as big a problem with her as I did before. But it still really bothers me how much influence she has over my dad. I just can't get used to that."

The guys went crazy again, booing the other team they were watching. They made so much noise that we all started laughing.

I sat back and looked at all my friends and got that feeling again that I was so lucky to have them.

It was so great to have everyone together again and happy.

It was really the most important thing in life.